Dont miss the rest of **RETURN TO FEAR STREET**

You May Now Kill the Bride

The Wrong Girl

RETURN TO FEAR STREET

DROP
DEAD
GORGEOUS

R.L. STINE

HARPER TEEN
An Imprint of HarperCollinsPublishers

HarperTeen is an imprint of HarperCollins Publishers.

Drop Dead Gorgeous

Library of Congress Control Number: 2018960535
ISBN 978-0-06-269429-4

Typography by Jenna Stempel-Lobell
18 19 20 21 22   PC/LSCH   10 9 8 7 6 5 4 3 2 1
❖
First Edition

To Kristen,
who has been a Fear Street resident since she was 19!

PART ONE

PART ONE

1

DEAR DIARY,

I'm always so happy to get back to you. The truth is, I never really feel like myself until I'm with you. It's as if I can reveal myself only to you.

I know I could write this on my phone, or maybe with one of those diary apps on my laptop. But I like the feel of your soft leather cover, the rich glow of your creamy paper, and the pen in my hand, the scratch on the paper that seems so real, so close from thoughts to words.

You are so close to me. You are my private listener, Diary. Away from all snoops. Away from everyone who might misunderstand me. It's so easy to eavesdrop online.

So let's start a new page. We are all about fresh starts, after all.

Yes, I'm excited. So many possibilities, so many dreams to fulfill, ambitions to achieve. And should I say danger to face?

A fresh start for me is all about new friends and experiences. New guys. New laughs. Even romance? What a quaint, old word.

I feel a warm glow as I think about this, Diary. I know I'm not a talented writer. I don't need to be a talented writer to tell you the truth of my life.

But fresh starts always give me this warm feeling, this tingle of excitement. So many new ways to satisfy yourself . . . to satisfy your hunger.

Yes, Diary, fresh starts mean so much more to you—when you are dead.

2

TOLD BY JULIE HART

"You *know* I can't serve you alcohol. You have to be twenty-one." The waitress was a lanky beanpole of a girl with stringy hair, watery brown eyes, and a tense, impatient frown on her face. Her name tag was pinned on upside down, but I could still read it: Jeannie. She tapped the iPad in her hand, eager to take our order.

"We're not here to drink," I said. "We're here to see Zane."

She blinked at me. "Who's Zane?"

"Our friend," I said. "He's doing a stand-up routine tonight."

"I'm laughing already," she said. She tapped the iPad some more.

"I'll just have fries and a Coke," Amber said.

"Is Pepsi okay?" the waitress asked.

"Sure."

Does anyone ever say no to that question?

I stared at the menu. "Can I have a cheeseburger?"

"You don't have to ask permission," Jeannie said. She tapped on the iPad.

"You're funny," Amber said. "Do you do stand-up, too?"

It was a logical question. We were sitting in Chuckles, after all. That's the only comedy club in Linden.

The waitress nodded. "Yeah. I do stand-up. I also do brain surgery. And I'm an astronaut." She turned to leave.

"Our friends are coming," I told her. "There will be five of us."

"Well, that just made my night," she said. She stepped up to another table, a table with three guys, and began tapping her iPad again.

Amber grinned at me. "I don't think she likes her job."

I laughed. "Is she the most sarcastic person in the world or what?"

It was a little after eight thirty and the club was filling up. I glanced around the tables, which were jammed tightly around the square room. They were filled mostly with twentysomethings. A lot of students, probably from the community college. Some couples holding hands over the small tables. Tall beer glasses at just about every table.

Amber and I were the only high school students that I could see. It was an eighteen-and-up club, and they were serious about not serving people under twenty-one.

The performers were adults, too. But Zane's cousin, Martin Finn, owns Chuckles, and he said Zane could come to open mic night and bring some of his friends.

Amber tangled a wisp of her brown hair, spinning it on a finger, then untangling it, then tangling it again. Amber is kind of a tense person, and that's one of her habits.

Actually, she hates her hair. Maybe that's why she tortures it. It's light brown and not really curly and not straight, either. She hates her hair, and she hates wearing glasses, and she thinks her nose is too long. She's always putting herself down, and if you try to say something nice, she says you're a liar.

"I look like an anteater next to you," Amber said to me once when we were standing in front of a mirror together. She tugged at her nose.

"I think anteaters are cute," I said, giving my blond hair a fluff.

"Shut up, Julie." That's her normal reply.

It's probably why we've been friends since third grade. Only really good friends can tell each other to shut up all the time.

I wish Amber could just calm down. She bites her nails, and tortures her hair, and I guess she's just not happy in her own skin. But she's a good friend. We really do care about one another.

And she's smart and serious and maybe the top student at Linden High. That has to count for something. For sure, she's gotten me through a lot of trig and chem tests. I'm not dumb—(yeah, dumb-blond joke here, ha-ha)—but I don't think I'd get the same grades without Amber's help.

Amber pushed her glasses up on her nose. "What made Zane want to do this anyway?" she asked.

"He's been writing his comedy act for weeks," I said.

"But what made him think he's funny? Zane isn't funny. He's so shy and quiet. He never cracks jokes in class."

I shrugged. "Beats me. It's just something he wanted to do."

"You're like his best friend," she said. "Didn't he explain it to you?"

"No. He says a lot of stand-ups are shy and quiet till they get onstage."

Amber bit her bottom lip. "Yeah, but what if he gets onstage and he's *still* shy and quiet?"

A middle-aged couple squeezed into the table next

to ours. Amber and I nodded hello. The man had a big belly poking out of his Hawaiian shirt, and he had a lot of trouble fitting it behind the small table.

"Liam should be the stand-up comic," Amber said. "Liam is funny."

I nodded. "Liam *is* funny. Funny-looking."

Amber grinned. "Do you think?"

Liam Franklin is an awesome guy. But his hair stands straight up on his head and his nose is like a bird beak. Add that to his tiny, round black eyes, he looks a lot like a rooster. Seriously.

And as we talked about him, Liam appeared. He slid through a line of people waiting for tables and dropped down across from me, beside Amber.

Despite the warm spring weather, Liam wore a heavy black leather jacket. He had a black-and-red Cleveland Indians baseball cap on backward.

"Hey, this place is crowded," he said. "I'll bet they all came to see Zane."

"For sure," I said.

"He's going to bomb big-time, isn't he?" Liam sighed.

Amber punched the sleeve of his jacket. "I thought you were Zane's friend. We're here to support him, right?"

Liam didn't answer. He unzipped the leather jacket

halfway, reached inside, and pulled out a bottle of white wine. "Some refreshment, courtesy of my parents, who don't know about it," he said, grinning.

"Did you bring a corkscrew, too?" I asked.

"It's a twist-off cap."

Amber glanced around. "We'll get caught."

"No one is watching," Liam insisted.

"They card everyone here," Amber said. "They're very strict. If we get caught—"

"If we get caught, they'll take it away from us." Liam shrugged.

"Did you bring cups or anything?" I asked. I saw the waitress walking toward us. She had our food on a tray.

"Wine tastes better right from the bottle," Liam said.

Amber squeezed his arm. "Hide it. Quick. Hide it! Here she comes."

Liam lowered the bottle to the floor between his legs.

Jeannie set down our order on the table. She turned to Liam. "What can I get you?"

"What beer do you have on draft?" Liam asked.

She squinted at him. "For you, I've got *root* beer."

"Sounds good," Liam said. "I'll have a cheeseburger, too. Can I have cheddar cheese?"

She stared at him. "Oh. You're a gourmet."

"Funny," Liam said.

"And the Indians suck," Jeannie said, squinting at his cap.

"You're just trying for a big tip," Liam said. We all laughed, even Jeannie. She turned and made her way back toward the kitchen.

Liam reached down to the floor and fumbled with the wine bottle. "I saw Delia and Winks outside," he said, motioning to the door with his head. "They were having a major fight, I think."

Delia Foreman and Winks are our other two friends. Winks's real name is Rich Winkleman, but no one calls him Rich, not even his parents.

Amber rolled her eyes. "So what else is new?"

"Yeah. They fight a lot," Liam agreed. He twisted off the wine-bottle cap and placed it on the table. Then he glanced around to see if anyone was looking, raised the bottle, and took a long sip.

He tried passing the bottle to Amber, but she waved no with both hands. I took it and had a quick taste. "Oh, yuck. That is *awful*! Are you sure that's wine? It tastes like *soap*!"

"Could be colder," Liam said. He took another drink and lowered the bottle to the floor.

"Delia is just too serious about Winks," Amber said, shaking her head."

"You're definitely right," I agreed. "I mean, how long have they been going together? A month? Maybe six weeks?"

Amber rolled a french fry between her fingers. "He is going to hurt her. I know he is."

"Nah. Winks is a good guy," Liam said. I could see he was checking out three very hot young women squeezed into a booth across from us.

"For sure he's a good guy," Amber said. "But he isn't serious like Delia. He doesn't have a serious bone in his body."

"True," Liam said, grinning. "But that's why he's a good guy."

"I tried to warn Delia about Winks," I said. "You know. Just trying to be helpful. I mean, Delia only moved here last fall. She doesn't really know anyone."

"Except us," Amber said.

"She seems so . . . helpless," I replied. "Innocent. I've been trying to take care of her a little."

Amber pushed her glasses up on her nose. "That's what I like about you, Julie. You want to take care of everyone."

Liam's eyes flashed. "Julie, would you like to take care of *me*?"

"Shut up, Liam."

He laughed.

Amber squeezed my arm. "So when you warned her about Winks, what did Delia say?"

"She told me to mind my own business."

Winks and Delia appeared across the club. They were holding hands, but they had these strained, phony smiles on their faces. Delia looked pale, and, even from halfway across the room, I could see that she had been crying.

Winks smiled when he saw us and came bouncing up to the table. He's a big, red-haired teddy bear of a guy, and his whole body bounces when he walks. He's open and friendly and loud and funny, lots of hugs and fist bumps, the kind of guy you like instantly when you see him.

They say opposites attract, and I think Delia is his opposite in many ways. She's shy and speaks in a whispery mouse voice. She's tiny and delicate, with pretty dark eyes and shiny black hair that falls in ringlets down to her shoulders.

"Hey, what's up?" Winks grabbed the wine bottle from between Liam's legs and took a long slug. He wiped some wine that ran down his chin with the back of his hand, then lowered the bottle to the floor.

Delia dropped into the chair next to me. "How's it going? You already ordered?"

"Yes. I—"

"You talk to Zane? Is he nervous?" Winks interrupted.

"I haven't seen him," I said. "They have a green room. You know. For the performers to hang out. He's back there."

"If he bombs, I'm outta here," Winks said. "I don't want to face him."

"If he bombs, we'll just tell him it was a bad crowd," Liam said.

We didn't have any more time to talk. The lights dimmed, and a spotlight swept over the small stage in front of us. A young guy wearing a blue-and-red Chuckles T-shirt over baggy denim jeans stepped onto the stage carrying a hand mic.

"Hey, everyone, I'm Stanley D and it's open mic night," he said. "You know what that means. You'd better drink up. It'll make these guys seem a whole lot funnier."

That got a small laugh.

"First up, we've got a very young comedian from Linden High North. He's so young, I had to *burp* him after his dinner! Let's give a Chuckles welcome to Zane Finn, everybody!"

Mild applause. Most people kept right on talking.

Zane stepped onto the stage and took the mic from the emcee. He was wearing his usual faded jeans ripped at both knees and a maroon T-shirt with big white letters that read: *DON'T JUDGE ME.*

He saw us. Our table was just to the side of the stage. He smiled at me. He didn't seem nervous at all. "Hello, everyone, I'm Zane," he said, raising the mic to his face. "Zane is an old biblical name that, I think, means, 'Do you want fries with that?' At least that's what my rabbi told me."

That got a good laugh.

I turned to see my friends' reactions. Whoa. Winks and Liam weren't even watching. Delia and Amber gazed up at Zane onstage. But the two boys were turned away, their attention somewhere else.

I turned and followed their gaze. It was easy to see what they were staring at.

A girl. A girl sitting by herself at the table behind us.

A beautiful girl with wavy copper-colored hair and big green eyes. High cheekbones like a model and dramatic red lips. Maybe the most gorgeous girl I'd ever seen. Beautiful, like from another planet.

Zane was into his routine onstage. But I was like Winks and Liam. I couldn't take my eyes off her.

And I couldn't stop thinking, *Why does she look so sad?*

3

JULIE HART CONTINUES

I forced myself to turn back to Zane. He had been calm and assured when he walked out. But now the mic trembled in his hand.

"Some people said I'm too young to be funny," he said. "But I think we're funny from the time we're born. I mean, what's funnier than pooping in your diaper?"

That got mild laughter. Someone in the back shouted, "Go change yours!"

Zane blinked but didn't reply. "My girlfriend didn't want me to go onstage," he continued. "She said I'm not good-looking enough. She said I have a good face for podcasts."

More polite titters.

I flashed him a thumbs-up to help encourage him. But I don't think he saw it.

Where was Zane looking? It took me a few seconds to realize he was gazing past our table. He had his eyes on that beautiful girl behind us.

He muffed his next joke completely. I could see he was distracted by her. I turned and saw that she was gazing up at him, too. But she wasn't laughing at his jokes. She wasn't even smiling.

Zane seemed to get shakier as he continued. Finally, he finished his act. "This was my first time onstage," he announced.

"Gee, we couldn't tell!" some guy shouted. It got a huge laugh.

Why are people so mean?

I could see the hurt in Zane's eyes. I wanted to rush onstage and give him a big hug.

"How would you rate me on a scale of ten to ten?" Zane asked the crowd.

Some people chuckled. The same guy shouted, "Minus ten!"

Zane waved good-bye, walked to the side of the stage, and handed the mic back to the host. He squeezed past a few tables and dropped down beside Amber with a loud sigh. "That went well," he murmured, shaking his head.

"I thought you were solid," I said. "I mean, for the first time."

He squinted at me. "Solid? What does *that* mean? What about funny?"

"That's what I meant," I said.

Zane tapped Winks's arm across the table. "What did you think? How was I?"

"Did you start yet?" Winks replied.

Amber slapped Winks's hand. "You're not funny."

Delia rolled her eyes. She sipped her Pepsi and didn't say anything.

"I'll bet her name is Darlene," Liam said.

I turned to him. "What are you talking about?"

The beautiful girl. She was shaking out her coppery hair, tossing her head as if she had just washed it.

"Why Darlene?" I asked.

"She's got to be a Jacqueline," Winks said. "But no one ever calls her Jackie."

"Have you both gone crazy?" Delia cried. "You've never seen a pretty girl before?"

"Not like that," Zane chimed in. "I think her name is Shannon. It goes with her red hair."

Amber grabbed my arm. "Let's go, Julie," she said, trying to pull me up. "We don't have to sit here and listen to these morons. They are obviously *hypnotized*."

Onstage, the emcee, Stanley D, waved for attention. "Hey, everyone, let's give our next performer a Chuckles welcome. By that, I mean totally ignore him! His name is Bernie Glaser, everyone. Here he comes. Feel the Bern! Feel the Bern!"

Bernie Glaser was maybe in his thirties, but looked older because he was balding and kind of stooped over, and had a large Adam's apple that bobbed at the neck of his gray turtleneck sweater.

"Can you imagine this? My girlfriend is so cheap," he started, "she'll only take me out to dinner two or three times a week."

Liam's chair clattered loudly as he jumped to his feet. The wine bottle on the floor started to topple over, but I caught it. "I'm going to ask her to come sit with us," Liam said. "I'll tell her we were betting on her name."

"Let's bet on whether she'll come over," Winks said. "I bet yes."

"I bet no," Delia said. "Look at her. You can see she wants to be alone."

"She hasn't smiled once," I said, watching her as she sipped a sparkling water. "She looks so sad. Don't bother her, Liam."

"My girlfriend is angry with me," Bernie Glaser said

up on the stage. "She caught me cheating on her with my wife."

Big laugh, mostly from the men.

Liam signaled to us with his fingers crossed. He rested his hand on Winks's head as he slid past and moved to the girl's table.

We all turned around to watch as he pulled out the chair and sat down across from her. Onstage, Bernie Glaser must have wondered what was going on.

Liam had his goofy grin pasted on his face, and he was talking a mile a minute.

The girl still didn't smile. But she didn't motion him away, either. A light beam from the stage caught her big green eyes and made them flash like emeralds.

Liam gestured to our table. We all quickly turned away. We didn't want to be caught staring.

"I think she's going to do it," Zane said. "I think she's going to come over here."

"Scoot over," Winks told Delia. "Make some room."

"You can make some room for my fist!" Delia exclaimed. The threat sounded funny in her mousy little voice. But I didn't think she was joking. She was totally possessive when it came to Winks. And the big idiot never really seemed to notice.

Then I saw the girl brush her hair off her shoulders

and stand up. She had a smile on her face for the first time.

"Whoa. Liam dropped the charm on her," Zane said. "Here she comes."

Yes. She adjusted her short black skirt and tugged down her silky green top as she followed Liam to our table.

And as I watched, I felt a chill.

A cold tightening at the back of my neck.

I put a warm, welcoming smile on my face. But I turned and whispered to Amber, "There's something strange about her."

Amber didn't react. She just kept her eyes on Liam and the girl as they approached.

"You know I'm always right about these things," I whispered. "I have a very bad feeling about this."

4

JULIE HART CONTINUES

Bernie Glaser finished his act with "Don't applaud. Just throw Bitcoins!" He walked offstage to mild applause and some scattered boos.

Liam dragged a chair up to the table and pushed it in next to his own. We all squeezed around and said hi as the girl gracefully lowered herself onto the chair and brushed her hair back again.

Liam dropped beside her and put an arm on the back of her chair, as if they were old friends or something. He had drops of perspiration on his forehead. He was really working hard to win her over.

I was directly across from her. And what totally blew me away was the smooth perfection of her skin, pale as cream and not a blemish, not a mark, as if she'd never been out in the sun for a minute. And I instantly noticed how the soft perfection of her skin made those enormous green eyes glow like jewels. It's a cliché, I know, but it's the only way to describe them.

We went around the table, announcing our names. Liam's hand tapped the back of her chair. "So is your name Darlene?" he asked.

I laughed. I couldn't believe Liam told her how we'd tried to guess her name by looking at her.

My laugh cut short when she said, "Yes. I'm Darlene."

Liam's eyes bulged. "Seriously? Are you seriously Darlene?"

"Not seriously," she said. She had a scratchy, hoarse voice, as if she hadn't used it for a while.

"But you are Darlene?" Liam wouldn't give up.

"Actually, no," she said. "I never knew a Darlene. Did you?"

"My cousin Darlene used to live a few blocks from me," Winks said. "But she moved to Houston."

"That's fascinating," Delia said sarcastically. She slid her arm through his and took his hand. She wanted to show the new girl that Winks was taken.

"My guess was Shannon," Zane said. "Was I close?"

She squeezed his hand. "Yes. Shannon. Good guess."

"You mean I was right?"

"No. My name is Morgan. Morgan Marks."

Zane groaned. "I saw you watching my act. What did you think?"

She shrugged her delicate shoulders. It made the silky material of her green top shimmer. "I'm the wrong person to ask," she said in that scratchy voice. "I don't get jokes. Really."

"Neither does Zane!" Liam joked.

We all laughed, everyone except Zane.

Morgan locked her eyes on Zane. She stared like she was burning into his brain. "Do you really want to be a comedian?"

"I just wanted to see what it feels like," he said.

She gave him a sly look. "You mean you like to try new experiences? That's bold."

Zane snickered. He looked uncomfortable.

He's so shy with girls. I've been coming on to him for years and he's never made a move. Now this beautiful girl was definitely flirting with him, and all he could do was snicker and blush.

"How about some wine?" Liam pulled the bottle off the floor. "It's a little warm . . ."

"No. But I'd like another LaCroix if you see the waitress."

Delia held on to Winks's arm. He had this big grin on

his face that looked painted on. He couldn't take his eyes off Morgan, and I could see Delia's features tightening as she became more and more annoyed with him.

"Are you new here?" I asked, trying to keep the conversation going so we didn't just have a staring match.

"I'm new everywhere," she replied. She smiled. "Does that make any sense?"

"You mean you just moved here?" Liam said. "Where is your house?"

She waved toward the door. "Somewhere over there."

Jeannie, the waitress, appeared. She narrowed her eyes at Zane. "I'd ask how you are doing, but I saw your act. Wish I could serve you a drink. I'm sure you need it."

Zane's face appeared to slump. "I was that good, huh?" he replied.

"No. Not *that* good," Jeannie said.

"You are *cold*," Winks said.

She frowned at him. "Keeping it real. Anybody want anything?"

I was still hungry. I ordered nachos for the table. We ordered more sodas. Morgan asked for another LaCroix.

"Where did you live before here? Where did you go to school?" Liam asked Morgan after Jeannie walked away.

She ran a finger down his sleeve. "You're very inquisitive, aren't you?"

Liam shrugged. "I just wondered . . ."

"I've moved around a lot," Morgan said. "Sometimes it's like a blur. I don't remember where I've been or where I'm coming from." She touched his arm again. "You ever have that feeling where you want to lose yourself completely and not know where you are?"

Liam hesitated. "Well . . ."

"Liam is *always* lost," Winks joked. I could see he didn't like all the attention Liam was getting from Morgan.

Zane just sat there staring at her. Like she was a new species. He seemed totally hypnotized.

Did she notice that all three boys were like deer caught in headlights, all three helplessly insane for her, ready to become her slaves, and she'd barely said a word?

I thought she did.

Amber and I exchanged glances across the table. We both saw that Morgan was a total flirt.

She had this way of letting her hair fall over her face and making her green eyes go wide when she concentrated on one of them. She used her hoarse voice to sound sexy.

And she was one of those people who touch you as she talks to you. She kept rubbing Liam's arm and touching his chest. She even reached across the table once to brush Zane's hair back from his forehead.

Delia eyed her warily. She had tightened her grip on Winks's arm and had pulled back her head, her expression tense, like a wildcat preparing to spring. Winks didn't seem aware of Delia at all. He kept grinning at Morgan and nodding at everything she said.

Which wasn't much. She seemed really swift at not answering questions or giving away anything about herself. We still didn't know where she came from or when she got to Linden or where she lived.

"Hey, how's it going?" A loud voice interrupted our conversation. I turned to see Bernie Glaser behind me, a tall drink in one hand. I saw a round spot on his gray turtleneck and guessed he had spilled some of the drink.

He reached across the table and bumped fists with Zane. "I watched your act, man. Not bad. I mean, for a first-timer."

Zane seemed embarrassed by the compliment. But he said, "Hey, thanks. I thought—"

"You were thinking too much, man," Glaser said. "I could see the gears spinning. You just got to let it go. Know what I mean?"

"I guess. I—"

"Well, see you around, guys." He raised his glass. "Cheers." He turned and walked away. His stoop-shouldered gait made him look a lot older than he was.

Liam turned back to Morgan. "Linden is a pretty big high school," he said. "It takes in all the surrounding communities. You might need some help navigating at first. I could help. . . ."

"That would be nice," Morgan purred.

"Liam gets lost all the time," Winks said again. "He can't find anything. He can't find his butt with both hands."

"Hey—!" Liam shouted. "Leave the jokes to Zane."

"Who's joking?" Winks said. He turned back to Morgan. "I could meet you Monday morning before homeroom."

"Sweet," Morgan murmured, doing her wide-eye thing.

Amber and I shared another disgusted look. Well . . . not really disgusted. It's just that Morgan was being so obvious, and the boys were being such jerks.

Finally, I turned to Morgan. "You said you don't like jokes?" I said.

She nodded. "It's just that I don't *get* jokes."

"Then why did you come here tonight?" I demanded.

Her smile faded. "Fresh blood," she said.

5

TOLD BY BERNIE GLASER

Twenty-five dollars and all I can drink. That's a good night for me. I'm not bitter or anything, but here I am, thirty-four years old, still driving a UPS truck, my bony knees in the brown shorts, my balding head sunburned from being outside all day . . . still getting my heart pumping at open mic night in a crummy falling-down comedy club in a nowhere town you can't even find on a map. At least, I couldn't find it if I hadn't been born here.

Born in captivity.

That's the real joke.

We're *all* born in captivity—aren't we?

I should put it in my act. It's about as funny as anything else I got.

All those jokes about my girlfriend, and I haven't had

a girlfriend since I had a full head of hair and all those big dreams of showbiz glory. Ha-ha. *Feel the Bern. Feel the Bern, everyone!* Not that I'm bitter.

You got to be bitter to be funny, right? At least it helps. You know. You've got to have an attitude. That's what comedy is all about. That attitude.

As if I know what I'm talking about.

Well, I know a good tequila and tonic. Or maybe three of them. I lost count. And now I'm walking to get the buzz off. Clear my head so I can drive back to my little studio apartment and wallow in pity till I fall asleep on the couch.

The fresh air feels so good on my hot cheeks. Of course, everything is closed up, even the Starbucks. They call this part of town Five Corners, and it's the only happening neighborhood in this existentially boring place. But, of course, it isn't *happening*, either. At least, not after ten o'clock at night.

A warm spring night and the soft bump of my shoes on the sidewalk is the only sound, except for the soft rustling of the trees in the little park across the street.

Aren't I poetic? Well, I wrote a lot of poetry when I was at Penn State. But I always tried to make it funny. You know, satiric, ironic. And who wants funny poetry? Everyone wants *sensitive*.

I step into the park. Maybe I'm weaving a bit, a little unsteady. But I want to get a sniff of those fresh trees, the leaves just uncurling, the spring grass so fragrant and sweet. Just a chill as I step under the trees.

And there is the girl. Is she waiting for me?

No. She couldn't be.

Her face gleams as pale as moonlight. No. The moon was never as beautiful. She glows, and her red-lipped smile spreads over that beautiful face, coppery hair catching the glint of light from the streetlamp behind us.

She moves toward me, her face open, like she's expecting something. Suddenly, I wish I had a clear head. But she smells sweet, like flowers, intoxicating . . . intoxicating.

I knew I was breathing fast. I shook my head hard, but it only sent a shooting pain down my neck.

"Hey," she whispered. So close now, the flowery scent wrapping me up.

"I—I saw you at the club," I stammered. "Did you follow me here?"

She tossed a wave of hair off her forehead. Her eyes were green and bright as traffic lights. She didn't answer. A teasing smile spread over her face.

"Did you like my act?" I asked. So lame. But usually my first question to anyone.

"I liked your act," she whispered. Her voice was soft and hoarse.

"Thank you," I said. Still lame. But my head cleared a little and I began to see that we were alone in this tiny, dark park. "What did you want? My autograph?" I actually made a joke.

Another teasing smile from her. "What do I want?" Pause. "You'll see."

She took my hand. Her fingers were ice-cold.

"No. Wait," I said. I suddenly imagined a Linden patrol car pulling up to the curb.

She ignored me and slid her hands across the front of my turtleneck. Chills. Believe me. Chills down my back.

"I liked your act, honey," she whispered.

"No. Wait." I tried to back up, but I was against a wide tree trunk. "How . . . how old are you?"

She brought her lips close to my ear. "Old enough," she whispered.

"No. Listen." I tried to gently push her back. "You're a beautiful girl. But I know you're not old enough. I saw you with those teenagers. You . . . you could get me in a whole lot of trouble."

She giggled. A light giggle, like a tinkling piano. "That's the idea."

And then her cold hands were wrapped around the

back of my neck, and she pulled my face to hers. And kissed me, softly at first and then with more energy, her lips moving on mine. And, yes, I kissed her back. I'm human, you know.

Her soft hair brushed my face. My heart started to pound. The kiss lasted a long time. I knew I was still buzzing, not from the drinks but from the flower-sweet fragrance and the fresh, cool air and the tingling feel of her hands on the back of my neck and the hard push of her lips against mine.

Intoxicating.

I stood there, my eyes half shut, my whole body tensed and pulsing. I didn't even open my eyes when she tugged down the neck of my turtleneck.

And pressed her lips against the pulsing vein in my throat.

I didn't make a sound until I felt her teeth pierce my skin . . . until I felt the stab of pain as two pinpricks at my throat became a roaring, drilling pain.

I tried to scream, but only a groan escaped my throat.

I guess I went into instant shock. So surprised . . . so taken unaware.

She made loud slurping sounds, and her tongue lapped against my neck. I could feel the warm liquid on my skin and beneath her tongue.

Helpless. I tried to squirm away. Tried to jerk my head from her teeth. But I was helpless. No longer intoxicated but under a spell, a strong spell that made me feel weaker . . . then weaker.

She lapped the flowing, hot liquid as it rolled down my neck. Her tongue darted along my skin. Slurping and gulping, she was no longer beautiful.

I pictured an old vampire movie. It was in black and white because the color was leaving my life. My *life* was leaving my life. And the scene from the old vampire movie with a full moon above and a dark-caped blood-drinker was the last thing I saw.

6

DEAR DIARY,

Who will be my number one guy?
Who will be first to take me high?
Who will be first to say good-bye?
Who will be the first—the first to die?

Diary, sometimes I get so hungry.
Nachos just won't do the trick. You know what I
mean. You know better than anyone.

The guys were so welcoming. The girls, too. My
new friends. I like being one of them, one of a gang,
one of a group. It's something I've always wanted, even
though I have to work so hard to be normal like them. I
have to rein myself in, put on a face, be someone else.

And they accepted me right away.

Ha. They don't know my game. They don't know so much that I know. Of course, I wish it were different. Of course, I wish . . .

I don't know what to write, Diary. I sat there with them in that comedy club, and I didn't feel like laughing. That was the last thing on my mind.

Winks and Zane and Liam. They were all overcome. Drooling like puppy dogs with their tongues hanging out. They were so obvious, so uncool. Like they didn't care what they looked like, how eager they were to impress.

When you're squeezed around a little table, all squeezed together, I have so much trouble keeping it together. Because I can hear the nectar flowing. I can hear the blood pulsing through their veins. And the sound starts a deep craving that is impossible to hold down.

But I have to be careful, Diary. I can't let my frustration show. I can't let anyone see my hunger.

Winks . . . Liam . . . Zane. I want to taste them all. And I will.

But, as it read on that old pillow in my mother's bedroom, "Patience is a virtue."

7

WINKS CONTINUES THE STORY

I'm a little early to school. Not sure how that happened. Obviously, I'm losing it. Most mornings, Mom has to shake me for five minutes before I'll open my eyes.

She says she's always afraid I'm dead. But I'm just a good sleeper.

I think everyone would like school a lot better if it started in the afternoon.

But here I am in the nearly empty halls of beautiful Linden High North. And am I surprised to hear running footsteps on the hard floor and someone shouting my name? Yes, I am.

It's Delia, and she seems to be angry yet again.

Like, give me a break just one morning, please. Don't get me wrong. She's hot and all that, and, hey, she obviously has a thing for the Big Guy. (That's yours truly, the one and only Winks.) So I put up with her. It's the nice thing to do.

I put a grin on my face, spin around, and hold out my arms. "Hey, sunshine! How about a morning hug?"

She makes a disgusted face. "Ugh."

Really. That's what she said. "Ugh."

Her hair fell in crazy ringlets around her face. It looked like it hadn't been brushed. Her eyes were narrowed at me angrily.

Delia is tiny like a mouse and has that whispery voice. But she can be a lion when she wants to be. *Roar.*

This morning, she wore a few layers of T-shirts, a navy blue one on top, and tight-legged jeans that looked like they came from the kiddie department. I told you: she's tiny.

She crossed her arms tightly over her chest and tapped one foot as she stared at me. I mean, I guessed she was staring at me. I couldn't see her eyes through the dark shades.

I sighed. "Okay. What did I do wrong this time?"

"Winks, you said you'd stop by my house and pick me up."

"Oh, wow." I slapped my forehead. "You're right. You're totally right."

Some kids drifted in and started banging open their lockers. The hall was filling up.

Delia uncrossed her arms and balled her hands into fists. "Don't you *ever* think about me?" she cried. "You woke up this morning and you came to school, and you never even *thought* about me?"

I motioned with both hands. "Please, Delia—not so loud. People are watching."

"Do I care?" she shouted. "I'm asking you a serious question. Do you ever think about me?"

"Of course," I said. I reached out to put my hand on her shoulder, but she backed away. "I think about you a lot."

"A lot? Only *a lot*?"

For some reason, that made us both laugh. It was a ridiculous conversation. I wasn't sure why she insisted on having conversations like this *all the time*.

And people *were* watching. I saw Liam at his locker, a questioning look on his face, like, *What's up with you two?*

"I'm sorry," I said to Delia. "I woke up too early this morning, and my brain never got into gear. I mean, I was so shocked at being awake before seven, I couldn't think of anything."

"That's the worst excuse I ever heard," Delia said.

But she didn't say it angrily. She had a tiny smile on her face.

I gave her a quick hug. She's so light. It's like hugging a butterfly.

We're not allowed to show affection or anything in the halls at school. Seriously. Not even a hug. It's in the rule book they give everyone on the first day of school.

Most everyone ignores the rule. But I know a few kids who were caught kissing—and had to go to Mrs. Hart's office and have a long, heartfelt discussion with her.

Our principal believes in having a lot of serious discussions with students. She says she's all about communication and transparency, whatever that means.

Actually, Mrs. Hart is okay. I've known her forever because she's Julie's mother.

Delia and I were standing across from the principal's office, and I saw Julie behind the front desk. She works in the office and helps her mother out.

Julie looked away when she saw me gazing at her, but I knew she'd been watching Delia and me have yet another argument.

Our parents are friends, so Julie and I have been thrown together for a lot of years. I guess she probably knows me better than anyone, which is weird, because I always have this feeling that she doesn't really approve of me.

Julie is kind of a straight arrow and, if you want the truth, not that much in the fun or sense-of-humor department. But we've been friends for so long, it's not like I can get out of it now.

I'm not a bad guy. She knows that. I don't really understand why she can be kind of cold sometimes. Ever since Delia arrived in school, Julie has worked hard to be her best friend.

I guess Julie thinks I don't care enough about Delia, and she's probably right. I mean, this girl seems to want to act like we're *married*.

So I hugged Delia, just a quick touch, and I said, "I have my mom's car. I'll take you to Benson's for lunch."

That's a special privilege if you're a senior. You can leave school at lunchtime.

Delia eats like a bird, seriously. Like a few seeds for lunch. But she likes Benson's, and I know she liked the idea of going off together at lunchtime because we don't do it very often. So she said yes and hurried away.

And then I had Liam beside me. I'd seen him watching us, and I knew he'd be coming over for details. Liam is one of my best buds, but he's a bit of a gossip. No one takes him seriously. He's definitely a player, and he likes to know what's going on, even if it isn't his business.

"So what's up with you and Delia?" he asked.

"Never mind," I said. "Are we up for a game on Saturday?"

Liam shrugged. "If we can find some guys."

Liam and I are totally into Ultimate Frisbee. I mean, we're major-league fanatics. We try to play every Saturday in the playground behind the middle school. But you need two teams, and sometimes it's hard to find dudes who want to play.

We've even tried Zane. That's how desperate we are. But Zane says he doesn't like to sweat, which is why he never plays sports unless he has to.

"So what was that about?" Liam demanded. I knew he wasn't going to give up.

"About five minutes," I said.

"Ha-ha. Good one. Remind me to laugh." He twisted his baseball cap around to face the back of his head. He wears it all the time because his hair is ridiculous. I mean, it won't stay down at all. It's like he's got porcupine hair or something.

We walked toward Mr. Deckland's homeroom. I gazed around to make sure Delia wasn't still hanging around. "Delia is in my face all the time," I said.

Liam nodded. "Are you going to break up with her?"

"We already have," I said, "but she doesn't know it."

What was I saying? I didn't know it, either. Had I just decided to break up with Delia at that moment?

"She'll be messed up," Liam said, scratching one side of his face. "Delia, like, thinks the two of you are married or something."

"Yeah. That's the problem."

It was too early to be thinking this hard. My brain usually stays in sleep mode till after lunch. I changed the subject back to Ultimate Frisbee.

Liam said he was working on getting a team together. Then he bumped fists with me and hurried away.

I turned a corner, into the hall that led to homeroom. I passed a group of cheerleaders in their blue-and-yellow uniforms. All very hot-looking in those pleated short skirts. They must have had an early-morning practice.

Basketball season was over. I wasn't sure what they were practicing for. Maybe just to keep in shape.

My friend Leesa is one of them. She led them all over to me. They surrounded me. Their faces glistened with sweat. Some of them were red-faced from their workout.

"Let's make up a cheer for Winks!" Leesa said.

They mostly reacted with laughter.

"Go, Winks! Go, Winks!" a girl named Min Lee shouted.

And then someone said, "What rhymes with Winks?"

Then they thought it was a riot when someone said, "Stinks." I think it was Leesa.

That ended the whole cheer thing. Believe me, I was loving the attention and hated to see them go.

I watched them until they turned the corner. Then I continued toward homeroom. I was just a few doors down when I felt a hand squeeze my arm.

"Winks?"

I spun around and gazed at Morgan Marks. Gazed right into those huge green eyes. Her hair was pulled back in a long ponytail. She wore a purple V-neck top that came down over a short black skirt.

"Winks, you know it's my first day. I'm lost. Can you help me find my homeroom?"

She smelled flowery, sweet. Most girls at Linden don't wear perfume or anything. But she was definitely different. The sweet aroma nearly made my eyes tear.

"Sure. No problem," I said.

"Oh, thank you." She reached for my arm again, and her purple fingernails scraped the skin.

I cried out in surprise.

"I-I'm sorry!" she stammered. "My hand slipped. I—"

"No worries," I said. I raised my arm to examine it.

"I scratched you," Morgan said. "Oh, wow. It was an accident. I'm so sorry."

Her fingernail had scratched a tiny line on my biceps under my T-shirt sleeve, and a few drops of bright red blood trickled along the line. "No big deal," I said.

But to my surprise, she reached out, pressed her pointer finger against my arm, rubbed the blood off the scratch. Then she raised her blood-covered finger to her lips—and licked the blood off.

Morgan's eyes flashed, and she grinned at me. "Now we're blood buddies," she said.

8

JULIE HART CONTINUES THE STORY

"Ow." I let out a cry.

"Julie? What's wrong?" Mom called from the inner office.

"Nothing. Just a paper cut," I said. I sucked on the finger. It wasn't going to bleed much.

Emily Hanes, the office secretary, looked up from her computer monitor. "Do you need a Band-Aid?" Emily has anything anyone would ever need in her desk drawer.

I shook my head. "I'm fine."

"You're going to be late for homeroom," Mom called. She laughed. "And I won't write you an excuse."

"Thanks a bunch." She thinks she's funny, and I guess she is. And it's hard to keep a sense of humor when you're principal of a high school, especially one as big as Linden North.

I started to close the file I was looking at, but Amber appeared, looking tense, her hair in disarray, as usual. "Hey," I said. "What's up?"

"My blood pressure." One of her jokes.

"Seventeen-year-olds don't have blood pressures," I said.

"Thank you, Nurse Julie." She banged her backpack on top of the front counter.

"I haven't seen you," I said. "Want to hang after school?"

She raked a hand through her hair. "Can't. I have a piano recital. I mean, a rehearsal for a recital."

"Cool," I said. "What are you playing?"

"Just some Chopin stuff."

I had to laugh. Amber is a brilliant pianist. Her teacher thinks she's a cinch to get into Juilliard, the famous music college in New York City. But Amber never wants to make a fuss about it and always plays it down like it's no big deal.

"You're going to be late, too," I said, glancing up at the big wall clock. "Why'd you come in here?"

"To tell you what I overheard."

I stared at her, waiting for her to continue. Finally, I had to say, "Go ahead. Spill."

She leaned over the counter and spoke just above a whisper. "Zane, Liam, and Winks were talking in front of Zane's locker, and I was just around the corner."

"And?"

"I wasn't eavesdropping or anything. I was just listening. And I heard them make a bet." She swallowed.

"A bet?"

"Yeah. They made a bet about which one of them will hook up with Morgan first. Do you believe that?"

I shook my head. "What are *we*? Chopped liver?"

She pushed her glasses up on her nose. "Tell me about it."

"Do you know how obvious I've been with Zane? I actually threw myself onto his lap and put my arms around his neck at Brian Dorsey's party. And Zane still thinks of us as pals. But Morgan comes along with that perfect angel face and—"

"I'm thinking about Delia," Amber interrupted. "If she knew that Winks was in a contest for another girl . . ."

The first bell rang.

Amber grabbed her backpack. "Gotta run. Later." She rocketed out of the office.

I stood there thinking about the guys and their bet.

Yes, Morgan is gorgeous. But, come on.

"You're late again." Mom appeared in her office door. She held a stack of blue folders in her hands. "Who were you talking to?"

"Amber. She just stopped by to—"

"We haven't seen Amber in a long time," Mom said. "You should invite her to dinner."

"She's always at a piano rehearsal," I said.

"She's a talented girl."

What did *that* mean? Was she saying that I'm *not* talented? Mom and I have all these discussions about how I don't have any hobbies or anything I'm passionate about.

Like that makes me a bad person.

Mom carried the blue folders over to Emily.

I thought about what Amber overheard. Three guys making a bet about Morgan. I had one more thing I wanted to do before I ran to homeroom.

I went into the student-profile files and typed in her name. The computers in the office are incredibly old and slow. They're like caveman computers.

I squinted at the screen. Was I spelling her name correctly?

I tried a different spelling. M-A-R-X? M-A-R-C-K-S? There aren't too many ways you can spell it.

"Julie, remember I have a meeting in Martinsville

after school, so I'll be home late," Mom said.

"Mom, take a look at this." I motioned her over.

"What's the problem?"

"Well . . . that new girl. Morgan Marks? Her school records aren't here. I can't find anything."

Mom lowered her face to the screen. She rubbed her chin. "Weird. She starts school today. The records are supposed to be on file before a new student can begin class."

"Yeah," I said. "Weird."

9

WINKS NARRATES

So I'm starting to drive home after school, pulling my mom's Camry out of the student parking lot, windows down on a warm, windy day. Feeling the fresh air on my face, starting to feel alive after sitting like a zombie in class all afternoon.

I've got my Pandora hip-hop channel cranked up, one hand on the wheel, other arm out the window. Life is good, yeah. Sure, I'd like my own car. A lot of kids at school get them on their seventeenth birthdays. But we can't afford it, especially since Mom was laid off after Christmas.

Not a bad day. Delia and I had a good lunch at Benson's and didn't fight about anything. Of course, we'd definitely fight if she could read my thoughts. Because I wasn't thinking about her much. I was thinking about

Morgan Marks and how I knew I could win the bet.

The Big Guy is adorable, after all. So cute and cuddly. Ha! Ask anyone.

And now, turning onto Parker Drive, I was thinking about being cute and cuddly with Morgan—*and there she was*!

Whoa. As if she could read my thoughts.

She was walking fast along the sidewalk, taking long strides, and her long red hair caught the sunlight and looked like a trail of fire behind her.

Man, was she turning me into a poet.

I pulled the car to the curb and cut the music off. "Hey, Morgan—" I leaned toward the open passenger window. "Want a ride?"

She took a few steps toward the car and lowered her head to see who was calling to her. Her hair blew wild about her face. Her green eyes peered in at me for a long moment. "No, thanks."

"Where do you live?" I called out.

"In a house."

"Well . . . where are you headed?" I asked.

"Somewhere."

She was teasing me. I loved it. I'd let her tease me all day, if she wanted.

"Morgan, do you know Linden at all? I could show you around."

Her eyes flashed. "I'll *bet* you could."

"No. Seriously."

She placed one hand on the passenger door and poked her head into the car. "Winks, you have a girl-friend, right?"

"Not . . . really," I said. My face suddenly felt hot. I hoped I wasn't blushing.

For some reason, that made her laugh. She laughed—and pulled open the car door. And then I could smell the flowery perfume that seemed to always accompany her as she dropped into the seat next to me. She pulled the car door shut and tried to smooth her hair down with both hands.

Then she turned to me and placed a hand on mine. "Winks, are you a good driver?"

"The *best*," I said. What else could I say? My mouth suddenly felt dry. Was my heart beating a little faster than normal? Maybe.

She was just so awesomely beautiful.

"Where do you want to go?" I asked.

An SUV rumbled past us, blowing its horn. I didn't turn to see who it was.

"Somewhere interesting," she said. Her hand was still on mine.

"Have you seen the lake?" I asked.

She shook her head. "I just moved here, Winks. I haven't seen anything." She motioned straight ahead with both hands. "Show me the lake."

I pulled away from the curb and lowered my foot on the gas. "The lake is called Parker Lake," I told her. "Just about everything in Linden is called Parker. I think they were the first rich people who moved here back in the day."

Morgan settled back in the seat. "Fascinating."

I knew she was being sarcastic, but I didn't care.

I didn't mention that Parker Lake is where couples from school go to park at night and hook up. And as I turned onto Lake Road, I suddenly remembered my after-school job. I was supposed to be at the car wash by four.

"There's the lake!" Morgan exclaimed. She seemed excited to see it. "Look at how the sunlight makes it sparkle," Morgan gushed. "Beautiful."

The road curved around. It looked like we were driving into the sun, which hung low over the water. I pulled the visor down. It was a little blinding.

She squeezed my arm. "Pull over. I want to see it."

I slowed down, but I didn't stop. "I . . . I don't have much time," I said.

"Pull over," she insisted.

I swerved hard and pulled the car onto the grassy shore. We were the only car there.

She leaned forward and gazed out through the windshield. The afternoon sunlight did make the lake sparkle. And beyond it, the woods appeared so bright and clear, you could see every tree.

"This is nice, but I really have to get moving," I said.

And then her hands were around my neck and she was pulling me to her. Her mouth crushed against mine. I actually cried out. It was such a hard collision.

She held my neck and moved her lips against mine. Kissed me. Kissed me. And I kissed her back. We held the kiss, one long kiss, until we were both breathless.

Then she slid her mouth against the side of my face, licking like a dog. Slid her tongue over my skin until my whole body tingled with excitement, my skin alive, chills down the back of my neck.

I could hardly breathe. But she lowered her lips to mine and we began another long kiss.

Is she crazy? I wondered.

I couldn't really think. I couldn't put words together.

Is she crazy?

Do I care?

10

WINKS CONTINUES

I don't even remember where I dropped her off. And, of course, I was late to the car wash.

My mouth felt swollen and dry. I could still taste her lips on mine. And my brain kept skipping around, like it was playing hopscotch or something.

I squinted hard and gritted my teeth, trying to steady myself, trying to get back to normal. But my racing heartbeat wouldn't let me. And I kept picturing that beautiful girl—a girl I didn't even know—and how hungry she was for me.

Hungry. That's definitely the word.

And I had to smile when I thought about how easy it was to win the bet with Liam and Zane. Because Morgan was obviously nuts about *me*. Too late for them.

They never stood a chance.

I pulled behind the neon Klean Kar sign at the front. I don't know why Dewey, the owner, decided to spell *clean* and *car* with *K*s. I think about it every time I arrive. I guess it's an attention getter.

Dewey is an okay guy, except if you're late. So I knew he'd be steamed at me and I'd hear about it. Several excuses flashed through my mind, but none of them sounded believable to me.

My brain was still spinning. I felt another chill when I remembered Morgan's hands on the back of my neck, pulling me toward her, holding me so tight I couldn't move, holding me for that endless kiss.

I'd seen a magician on TV hypnotize some people. And when he finally let them come out of it, they were all groggy and weird. And that's just what I felt like. Weird. Off, somehow.

I cut the engine and pocketed the keys and stepped unsteadily out of the car. A blue SUV had just come through the wash, but I didn't see anyone there to hand-dry it.

Where was Dewey?

Then I saw a tall, strange-looking dude walking across the lot toward me. He had short white-blond hair spiked up in a strip in the middle of his head. And as he came close, I could see that his eyes were like silver and trained hard on me.

He was ripped, big chest, big biceps. Dressed like a tough guy in a tight, black, sleeveless shirt, black jeans tucked into tall boots. The heels of the boots made loud *bumps* on the pavement as he made his way toward me with slow, steady strides.

"Hey," I said.

I suddenly felt a little afraid. I guess it was the weird silver eyes. I mean, who has eyes with practically no color at all? A robot?

I looked for Dewey. But there was no sign of him. The blue SUV pulled away, and the dude and I were alone now.

"My name is Cal," he said, and to my surprise, he had a normal, smooth voice. "We've never met. I'm Delia's stepbrother."

Huh? Delia never mentioned a stepbrother.

"Oh. Hi," I said. "I'm Rich. Everyone calls me Winks."

He nodded. The sunlight gleamed off his spiky hair. "I know. I have something for you, Winks."

Before I could react, he shot his right hand forward—and landed his fist hard in the pit of my stomach.

I made an *ooof* sound as the breath poured out of me.

And then the pain shot up from my belly, up to my arms, my head. And I threw my arms around myself and doubled over, groaning, choking, gasping for breath.

When I finally straightened up, he had the power hose in his hands.

"Hey, wait—" My voice came out in a hoarse whisper. "Please—"

The blast of water from the hose sent me stumbling backward. I tried to shield myself with both arms, but the spray from the hose was powerful enough to send me sprawling.

"Stop! Please—" I pleaded.

But he moved forward, moved with me, keeping the blast of water on my chest. Until I stumbled into the car wash.

I toppled into one wall, and the brushes started up, battering me, shoving me hard from side to side. I was helpless. Stumbling. I raised my hands to shield my face. And then I was choking on soapsuds.

"Please— Wait—"

One of the brushes scraped my side. My clothes were drenched. The soap bubbled around me. I frantically struggled to wipe burning suds from my eyes.

Oh, help.

The power brushes whirred and tore at my shirt. I

heard a rush of air. The cycle changed, and steaming hot water sprayed down from above. The shock took my breath away. I began to choke and gag.

"Can't breathe. Hey—I can't breathe."

I felt a hand grasp the soaked shoulder of my shirt. Cal dragged me out. Pushed me hard against the wall at the side of the building. I hunched against the concrete, brushing suds from my face, struggling to catch my breath.

"That was for Delia," Cal said, calm as a clam, as if we were just having a quiet conversation. "Like I said, she's my stepsister, and you'd better start treating her right."

"But I—"

Cal pushed me back against the wall with one fist. His silvery eyes glared into mine. "She's been through a lot, man. You've got to be careful with her. I was there at school to pick her up. I saw you drive off with that redheaded girl."

"Whoa. Listen—" I didn't know what I was going to say to the guy. I just knew I had to protest.

Cal raised a finger and pointed it at me. "This was a warning."

I took a deep breath and finally found my voice. "Are you *crazy*?" I cried. "You *attacked* me? Now you're *threatening* me? Are you totally crazy?"

He didn't answer. Just gave me one more push against the wall. "Stay away from that new girl," he murmured through his teeth. Then he turned and stomped away.

I stood there, soaked and shivering. My stomach ached from the punch he threw. My eyes burned from the soapsuds.

I've got to break up with Delia, I decided. *Her step-brother is nuts. And dangerous. And out of control.*

I heard my name being shouted. I turned and saw Dewey calling to me. How long had he been shouting?

I shook water off as I forced myself away from the wall and headed toward Dewey, who was outside the front office. My sneakers squished across the pavement. I brushed my wet hair back off my forehead.

Dewey is a big, brawny guy who wears red-and-black flannel shirts and denim bib overalls that make him look like a lumberjack. He has a lumberjack beard, too, black and thick, and long enough to cover his face and neck.

He did not look pleased. I could see his angry scowl even through his beard. "Winks—why are you soaking wet?"

"Did you see that guy?" I pointed toward the street.

"No. I was in back."

"That guy just came up and beat the crap out of me."

Dewey eyed me skeptically. "How come?"

"Beats me, Dewey. Seriously."

"Well, I have to shut down," he said, rubbing his beard. "You wrecked the whole mechanism."

"Huh?" I gasped. "It wasn't my fault. I—"

"You smashed everything up, Winks. I've got to shut down till I can get it fixed."

"But, Dewey—" I pleaded. "The guy threw me in there. You can't blame me."

"Who else am I going to blame?" Dewey didn't raise his voice, but he couldn't hide his anger. "Listen, Winks. You came late to work and then you wrecked the whole car wash. What would you suggest I do?"

"Give me another chance?"

"I don't think so. I think I have to fire you."

I couldn't think of a reply. Finally, I just nodded.

"I'll give you a check for last week," Dewey said. He turned and started into the office. "Don't come in the office. You'll get everything wet."

So I waited outside for him, hugging myself to stop the shivers and thinking, *The next time I see Cal, I'm going to tear him apart.*

11

AMBER NARRATES

"So you'll never guess Liam's new project," I said.

Julie turned to me. "New project? Since when does Liam have a project? His only projects are playing Ultimate Frisbee with Winks and seeing how many girls he can impress."

I mopped sweat off my forehead with the sleeve of my T-shirt and slowed my pace on the stationery bike. We were in Julie's basement, where her parents have their own gym setup. Julie was beside me on the treadmill, walking pretty slow because she wasn't in the mood.

Which was weird for Julie, because she's always in the mood to do *everything*. Julie is the most energetic, gung ho person I know. And I wasn't used to seeing her be so low energy.

But I had a pretty good idea why she was down. She'd told me she saw Zane hanging out with Morgan Marks in Franklin Park behind the high school, and I guess they looked pretty friendly.

If Zane and Morgan become a thing, it serves Julie right. Of course, I would never say that to her. But she is totally bold in everything else. Why can't she just walk up to Zane and say, "Hey, I have a thing for you."

Why is she so paralyzed when it comes to him?

It's easy for me to ask questions like that, I guess. But you think you know someone really well. I mean, Julie and I have been best friends since forever. But there are still mysteries about her I just can't crack.

"Liam is building a drone," I said.

Julie laughed and almost stumbled off the treadmill.

I pushed my glasses up on my nose. "No. Really," I said. "You know his uncle who is an engineer at Boeing? He sent Liam a kit. And Liam is building a drone in his garage."

"What for?" Julie said. "Does it have a camera? Does he want to spy on the girls' field hockey team?"

We both laughed. That seemed like the only logical reason Liam would build a drone.

I stopped pedaling. My thigh muscles were throbbing. I mopped my forehead again and climbed off the bike. My hair was sweaty, and it gets totally curled up when it's wet. "Hot in your basement," I said. "I feel virtuous enough."

"Yeah. Let's go upstairs and get something to drink."

A few minutes later, we were sprawled in her den, sitting cross-legged across from one another on the dark shag rug, sipping from cans of Diet Coke, with a bowl of nacho chips between us, a reward for our strenuous workout.

I decided to tell Julie my idea about Morgan. "I want to interview her for the *Panther Roar Blog*," I said. I'm one of the main writers for the school blog.

Julie swallowed some chips and squinted at me. "Interview Morgan? Why? For beauty tips? Think she can tell everyone how to look as gorgeous as she does?"

I laughed. "I don't think so." I paused. "Although come to think of it, some tips from her might be interesting." I sighed. "You know, my mom says I can't do anything about my nose until I'm eighteen. How unfair is that? Why do I have to walk around with this bird beak till I'm eighteen? It . . . it's ruining my life, and she doesn't care."

Julie set down her Diet Coke can and took my hand. "Amber, I've told you a hundred times, your nose isn't ugly. It's actually quite beautiful. Seriously."

I jerked my hand away. "Shut up. You're a liar, Julie. You've always been a liar."

"And you're crazy to be so obsessed with your nose."

"You'd be obsessed, too, if your nose entered the room five seconds before you did!"

We both laughed, and it cut the tension. Julie and I are so close, we have honest moments like that all the time. And no hurt feelings. Although I knew she was lying about my nose.

"Hey, we were talking about Morgan," I said. "Writing her up for the blog. She's new in school, right? And I just thought . . . well . . . the rest of us have lived here forever. Maybe it would be interesting to get her impressions on how it feels to be a new girl at Linden."

Julie rolled her eyes. "A new girl who looks like a movie star and has three guys panting after her like starving dogs."

I took a handful of chips. "You think it's a bad idea?"

Julie pushed a strand of blond hair off her face. "No. I didn't say that. Morgan might not want to do it, you know. She seems kind of private."

"Well, it doesn't hurt to try—"

"We don't know a thing about her," Julie said. "Mom doesn't even have her old school records at her office. It's like she popped in here from another planet."

"Well, you *know* I like sci-fi," I said. "I'm going to give it a try."

When I caught up with Morgan in the hall after school the next day, she said no.

"Why should anyone care about me?" she said.

"You're the only new student in our class this semester," I told her. "People have noticed you, right? So they'll want to read what you have to say."

"But I don't have anything to say." Her voice became shrill, kind of whiny.

"Why don't we just try it?" I said. "It'll only take a few minutes. I promise." Then I added, "I'd like to get to know you better. You don't really know anyone here, do you?"

Her expression softened. Her eyes studied me as if seeing me for the first time. "Okay," she said. "For only a few minutes?"

"Awesome!" I felt as if I'd won a big victory.

"When do you want to do it?" Morgan asked. "Now?"

That's how we ended up in the art room on the second floor. Empty. Smelling of paint and turpentine. Sitting across from each other at the end of a long worktable.

Morgan slipped off her silky green jacket and hung

it on the seatback next to her. I pulled out my phone and set it to record our conversation.

She fumbled in her bag, pulled out a silver lipstick case, and applied a bright purple color to her lips. "Can't do an interview without lipstick, right?"

"That reminds me," I said, positioning the phone between us on the table, "I'll need to snap a photo when we're done talking."

She shook her hair off her shoulders. "No problem."

"Before we start, I just wanted to ask you . . . Have you ever done any modeling? You're so beautiful, I'd think—"

Her eyes went wide. "Do you *really* think I'm beautiful?"

Her reaction stunned me. I just sat there staring at her. "Well . . . yes," I said finally.

"I've never done any modeling or anything," she said, turning her gaze to the tall windows across from us. "Never really thought about it."

I studied her face. Was she lying? She *had* to know she was gorgeous. Even if she didn't see it in the mirror, she'd know it from the ridiculous reactions of the guys around her.

Was she putting me on?

I took a breath. "Sorry. That question wasn't part of the interview." I turned the phone toward her. "So what are your first impressions of Linden High North?"

She smiled. "That it's big."

"Bigger than your old school?"

She nodded. "It seems like a whole *city* to me. And I feel like I'm walking down streets I've never seen before, and I don't have a map, and I don't know where I'm going."

"So you've found it kind of overwhelming?" I asked.

She nodded again. "Kind of. But everyone has been really helpful to me."

I shifted my weight on the bench. "That was my next question, Morgan. What do you think of the students here?"

She tilted her head to one side, as if thinking about her answer. "Well, you know, I came to town just a few weeks ago, but everyone seems very friendly, and I think there's a very relaxed vibe here. Like we're all in it together. That kind of thing."

What a phony.

A relaxed vibe? At Linden? Kids here eat each other for lunch!

Of course, I resented Morgan for being so beautiful.

But I was really trying to like her. I was serious about wanting to be her friend.

But she wasn't even *trying* to make me believe what she was saying. She had this grin on her face, and she kept looking to the window, avoiding my gaze.

"Has anyone been especially helpful to you?" I asked.

"A lot of people. They've been terrific when I'm lost and wandering the halls. Or in class when I'm not up with the assignments because I just got here."

She sighed and ran a hand back through her long hair. "Changing schools is a bummer, especially senior year. It's tough. I miss my old friends. Sometimes I feel . . . lonely. But everyone here has been great."

"Why did you have to change schools senior year?" I asked, desperate to get her to say something interesting.

"Oh, different things," she said, still playing with her hair. "A lot of reasons."

"What was your old school, Morgan? Where were you living?"

"Up north."

"No. Come on. What was the *name* of your old high school?"

She flashed that grin again. "You wouldn't recognize it."

She was playing me. And there was no way I could

win if she wasn't going to cooperate and give me good answers.

Shadows shifted outside the window. It was getting late. The afternoon sun was dropping behind the trees.

Out in the hall, I heard the shuffle of feet and a cough. I looked to the door, but I couldn't see anyone out there.

I took a deep breath and tried again. "Morgan, now that you are here at Linden, what are you looking forward to?"

"Graduation." She laughed.

"Well . . ." I tried to keep my frustration from my voice. "Is there anything you're particularly interested in? I mean, something you like to study? Something you are *passionate* about, as our teachers like to say?"

"Oh, just this and that," she replied. "You know. The usual."

That was all I could take. I jumped to my feet, making the bench scrape loudly against the floor. "Hey, thanks," I said. "Thanks for talking to me. I think I have everything I need."

She lowered her eyes and shook her head. "I told you I wouldn't be good at it."

"It was okay," I lied. I clicked off my phone and slid it into my bag.

She stood up and pulled her sweater down over her

short skirt. "Do you want to take a photo?"

"Sure," I said. I pointed to the wall, which was covered with framed artwork by students. "Stand over there."

She put a radiant smile on her face and opened her eyes wide, and I snapped a few shots. I didn't bother to look at them. I knew I'd probably never use them. The interview was too "nothing" to write up.

"Thanks again," I called as Morgan hurried to the door, dragging her jacket in one hand.

I heard someone greet her in the hall. A familiar voice. I peeked out and saw Liam with an arm around her shoulders, leading her to the stairs.

Liam had waited for her. Morgan and Liam.

And Julie had seen Morgan with Zane. And Morgan had also been hanging with Winks. Everyone but Delia knew that.

Gee. Are three guys enough for her?

Of course, it was my jealousy that made me think that.

I made my way downstairs and was heading to the front doors when I heard someone humming in the principal's office. I stepped inside and saw Julie sorting a big stack of papers at the front desk.

"Amber, hey!" She looked up, surprised to see me at school so late.

I dropped my backpack onto the floor. "I just did my blog interview with Morgan."

"How'd it go? You don't look happy."

"It didn't go," I said. "It sank. She was unbelievable, Julie. She wouldn't give me a straight answer on a single question. It was like a game she was playing. Agree to the interview and then reveal nothing about yourself."

"I warned you—" Julie started.

"She wouldn't even tell me what school she used to go to!" I cried.

"Funny you should mention that." Julie picked up a large brown envelope. "These are Morgan's records from her old school. They just came in. I haven't even opened them."

I grabbed for them, but Julie swiped them out of my reach. "Come on. Open them. Let's take a look," I said.

Julie scrunched up her face, the way she does when she's thinking hard. "We can't look at them," she said. "It's against the rules. You know, privacy rules." She glanced toward her mother's office. The light was out. Mrs. Hart wasn't there.

"Julie, open the envelope," I insisted. "There's no one here. No one will know if we take a quick peek. Aren't you curious?"

She hesitated, then tore off the top of the envelope. I saw a red file. And a white envelope.

Julie pulled out the envelope. It was addressed to her mother. She opened it carefully and pulled out a folded sheet of stationery.

"What does it say?" I demanded. "Come on. Read it."

She unfolded the paper and raised it to her face. "It's a letter," she said. "From the principal at Shadyside High School."

"Shadyside? Where is that?"

Julie didn't answer. Her eyes were scanning the letter. I watched as her mouth dropped open and she murmured, "Oh. Oh wow."

She dropped the letter onto the counter and raised her eyes to me. "Amber, I . . . really don't believe this." She raised the letter again. "The principal at this school . . . He says that Morgan Marks died five years ago."

PART TWO

PART TWO

12

LIAM CONTINUES THE STORY

Morgan isn't the first totally hot girl to want to get close to me. Maybe I'm bragging. But if you've got it, flaunt it. At least, that's what I've heard people say.

Girls fall all over me, and it's not because of my awesome good looks or my bod. It's simple. Girls like me because I'm really *into girls.*

Winks may be a big cuddly teddy bear, and Zane is a serious dude who is driven and ambitious. He says he wants to do comedy, but he almost never smiles. He always looks like someone just murdered his puppy.

I, on the other hand, am romance personified. So when I told Morgan I was building a drone in my garage, I knew she'd want to see it. How could she resist?

Her big green eyes went wide, and she gazed at me as if I was some kind of brilliant scientist. "You're really building a drone? By yourself? Can I see it?"

I played the modest game. "It's nothing, really. No biggie."

Hard for me to be modest, but sometimes I can pull it off.

We made a plan to meet after school. I didn't know that Amber was going to kidnap Morgan and interview her in the art room. So I waited out in the hall.

The school emptied out pretty fast. I sprawled on the floor with my back against the wall and texted Winks. I still hadn't rounded up enough guys for our Ultimate Frisbee game on Saturday. I wondered if he had any ideas.

I could hear Morgan and Amber mumble on inside the art room. Amber was pounding her with questions. I wished I could hear the answers. But they were at the far end of the room away from the door, and I just heard mumbling.

When she finally came out, Morgan was surprised to see me. And the big smile on her face told me she was pleased. "You didn't have to wait," she said.

"For sure I did," I said. "How was the interview?"

She shrugged as she pulled on her jacket. "Amber just wanted my impressions. I don't really have any yet. I mean, *you're* one of the few people I've met. And I don't know you very well, do I?"

She said it kind of in a sexy way, like she was teasing me or something.

"We can fix that," I said. Awkward. That sounded like some dude in a stupid rom-com movie. "Hey, you still want to see my drone?"

She laughed. "Best offer I've had all day."

So we ended up in my garage, and, of course, I've just started to put the thing together. I had some of the support rods connected. And I showed her the rest of the kit and the two engines.

She grabbed my arm and kind of squeezed me against her. I guess she was impressed. Her soft hair brushed my face and sent shivers down my whole body.

"What are you going to do with it?" she asked.

"Fly it to Mars," I said. "It should make a Mars landing in about a million light-years."

She laughed. "No. Really."

"Buzz the neighborhood with it and annoy everyone," I said.

"Sounds like a plan." She picked up a Frisbee and spun it in her hand. "Are you seriously into science?"

"No. I'm seriously into wasting time," I said.

She tossed the Frisbee at my chest. I think she wanted

to catch me by surprise, but I caught it easily. "Lightning reflexes," I said.

Her eyes flashed. "I'm impressed."

I pulled out my phone. "A quick selfie?"

She pressed herself against me again, bringing her face close to mine, and I snapped a few photos.

Then she was hungry, and so was I. I led the way into the house.

"Mom was supposed to make pizza tonight," I said.

Morgan examined the round glob of dough covered with wax paper on the counter. "You make homemade pizza?"

I nodded. "We have it a lot. My parents love gadgets and things. They bought this special pan that makes it really crispy."

"Cool," Morgan said.

"But they're not here," I explained. "They had to go visit my great-aunt in Pearson Falls."

"Well . . . can we make the pizza without them?" Morgan asked. She lifted the dough from the wax paper and began to knead it in her hands. "I'm a really good cook."

I squinted at her. "Seriously?"

"No. I'm lying. Sorry."

We both laughed.

I clicked the oven on. You need a very high oven

temperature for pizza. Then I found the mozzarella cheese in the fridge. Mom had already grated it. It was ready to spread on the dough. And I pulled out a thin salami. We always have this very spicy Sopressata salami on our pizzas.

Morgan slid a big knife from the wooden holder on the counter. "I like to slice," she said. "You do the cheese, and I'll slice the salami."

"Hey, we're a team!" I said. "Maybe we should go on Food Network."

I started to spread the cheese with my fingers. I'm not quite sure how it happened. But I let out a cry when I felt a sharp stab of pain at my wrist.

I spun around. Morgan had the knife in the air. I saw bright red blood trickle out from a cut on my wrist.

"Oh no!" she cried. "Oh no. I'm sorry, Liam. It slipped. The knife slipped."

"It's okay," I said. Actually, it hurt a lot. And the blood was oozing over my hand.

"I'm so sorry. I'm such a klutz." She set the knife down and grabbed my hand. She brought my wrist up close to her face. Then she raised those amazing eyes to me.

"I . . . I have a thing about blood," she said. She lowered her gaze to the bright red pool on my hand. "That's disturbing, right? But . . . I can't help it. It's so . . . basic."

"I . . . well . . ." I didn't know what to say. I started to reach for the paper towels, but she held on to my wrist.

And then I kind of gasped when she licked my wrist. Just a quick lick, and when she raised her head, she had my blood on her lips.

Then she leaned forward—and kissed me.

She pressed her lips hard against mine, and I could taste the blood. I could taste it as I kissed her, and we held the kiss for the longest time, her warm lips and the metal taste of my blood. My brain was spinning.

And I thought, *I won. Winks and Zane, I won the bet.*

When Morgan left, I pulled out my phone. I wanted to check out the selfies we took in the garage. My proof. My proof that I was the winner.

I raised the phone and hit the Photos app. And gazed at the first photo, then the next, then the next. "Whoa. What's up with this?" I murmured aloud.

I had this big grin on my face in each photo. There I was, grinning into the camera. But where was Morgan? The space next to me was empty. Morgan was missing. She wasn't in any of the photos.

13

JULIE NARRATES

"I don't know what's going on with Winks," Delia said, shaking her head. Her black ringlets bounced around her shoulders. She had her shades on, so I couldn't see her eyes.

"Did you two have another fight?" Amber asked. She spun the saltshaker between her hands. Amber was so tense, she always had to be doing something with her hands.

We were sitting in a red vinyl booth against the wall at Benson's. It was dinnertime, and we were lucky to get a seat.

Benson's is always crowded because the cheeseburgers are awesome—and because it's been the main hangout for Linden High kids ever since anyone can remember.

It was noisy and hot in the restaurant. People in twos

and threes stood by the front door, waiting for a table or booth to open up.

"We didn't have a fight," Delia said. "I think everything is okay between Winks and me." She sighed. "That's the good news."

"And what's the bad news?" I asked.

She pulled off her shades and dropped them onto the table. "Someone beat Winks up, and he lost his job at the car wash."

"Huh?" I gasped.

"Who beat Winks up?" Amber and I said in unison.

Delia shrugged. "He won't talk about it."

Amber squinted at her. "He won't tell you who it was?"

"Or what it was about?" I added.

"No. Not a word. He told me to stop asking about it. And he's been in a rotten mood ever since."

"I don't blame him," I said. "Was he badly hurt?"

"I don't think so," Delia replied. "But I can barely get a word out of him."

Amber snickered. "Which is worse? Winks fighting with you all the time? Or Winks giving you the silent treatment?"

I think Amber was trying to be light, but Delia wasn't in the mood. "He is usually such a fun guy. . . ." Her voice trailed off.

The waitress brought our food on a big tray. There was some confusion over who ordered the rare cheeseburger and who ordered the turkey burger. But we got it straightened around, and I didn't wait to dig in. I was hungry.

Amber wiped cheeseburger grease off her chin. "Did you know that Winks and Zane are helping Liam build a drone?"

"A real one or a Lego one?" I asked. They laughed.

"It's a horror story," Amber said. "Can you imagine all the trouble those guys can cause with a drone?"

"They'll probably crash it into a jet plane or something," Delia said.

I narrowed my eyes at her. "Whoa. That's pretty dark."

"Sorry. Just my mood." She nibbled at her turkey burger. I never saw anyone take such small bites.

"I'm sure they'll annoy people with it," I said. "You know. Buzz their lawns or take photos from outside the neighbors' bedroom windows."

"For sure," Amber agreed.

"How can those guys build a drone?" I asked. "They wouldn't know a Crescent wrench from linemen's pliers."

My friends stopped eating to stare at me. "How do *you* know those things?" Amber said.

"My dad is a mechanic, remember?" I said.

"I think Liam has a kit," Delia said. "That's what Winks told me. You know. Like a model kit. Only it's a real thing."

We ate in silence for a while. I finished the last fry and wished I had more. Delia still had a full plate of them. I reached across the table and took a handful of hers.

"Guess who waited a long time after school for Morgan Marks?" Amber said.

"Every guy in school?" I joked.

She shook her head. "I did that blog interview with Morgan," Amber continued. "Or at least, I tried. We were there nearly an hour, and when she left, I saw Liam waiting for her. They walked off holding hands."

"Morgan and Liam?" Delia seemed surprised.

Amber and I knew about the bet the three guys had made about which one could get with Morgan. But Delia didn't know. She'd be hurt that Winks had joined in.

All along, I'd been debating whether to bring up what Amber and I had learned about Morgan Marks. I knew it was private information that we shouldn't share. But I just couldn't help myself. It was too . . . weird.

I leaned across the table and lowered my voice. "I know I shouldn't talk about this . . . ," I said.

"Oh, good. You've got more gossip!" Amber exclaimed. Delia eyed me warily.

"You already know some of this," I told Amber. "You were in the office with me, remember?"

Amber nodded. "Oh, yeah. You mean about Morgan?"

"What about Morgan?" Delia demanded.

"There must be a mistake in her school records," I said. "My mom requested them from her old school and they arrived the other day. There was a letter that said Morgan *died five years ago*."

Delia blinked a few times. Finally, she said, "Well . . . she *is* very pale." I think she meant it as a joke. Amber and I both laughed.

"If I could be *that* gorgeous," Amber said, "I wouldn't mind being dead."

Amber and Delia laughed.

I didn't. "It really isn't a joke," I said. "I mean, I thought it was just a mix-up. It *had* to be a mix-up. What else? But . . . I googled Morgan Marks. And guess what? I found a bunch of news reports. She died in a car accident five years ago."

A long silence. Then Delia said, "So . . . she's like the living dead? A zombie? She doesn't *look* like a zombie, Julie."

"Let's ask her," Amber said. "She just walked in."

14

JULIE CONTINUES TO NARRATE

I turned toward the front door and saw Morgan enter, followed by Zane. They both glanced around, searching for an empty table. They didn't see us against the wall.

"Morgan and Zane?" Delia said to Amber. "I thought you saw her with Liam."

"I did," Amber said.

They both looked at me. They both know how I feel about Zane. And yes, it hurt to see him holding Morgan's hand, being so cozy with her as they slid into a booth at the back. It made me angry at myself that I'd been so timid all this time, that I'd been so stupid about not letting Zane know that I had a thing for him.

"Julie, where are you going?" Amber asked.

I didn't even realize I had jumped to my feet. "Uh . . . Let's say hi."

Amber slid out of the booth. "I'll stay here," Delia said. "They might take away the booth." She slid the dark glasses over her eyes. But before she did, I thought I glimpsed a tremor of fear.

What did Delia have to be afraid of?

Amber and I pushed through some kids who were moving to leave, and strode toward Morgan and Zane. They were laughing together about something but stopped when they saw us coming.

"Hey." Zane gave us a wave. He had a silly grin on his normally serious face. His dark eyes locked on mine. "How's it going?"

"Good," I said. "Delia's here, too." I motioned to our booth. "We're just finishing up."

"What did you have? A cheeseburger?" Zane laughed. It was kind of a private joke we always made. Because, what else would you have at Benson's?

I guess it was only funny to us. Zane and I had a lot of private jokes. And I just remembered I'd offered to help him with some new stuff for his comedy routine.

Morgan and Amber were talking about their blog interview. Morgan said, "We should try it again. I was totally spaced out that afternoon. I'm really sorry."

Amber said she'd love to do it over again some time. I was pretty sure she was lying.

I asked Zane when he wanted to work on his stand-up routine. We made a date for the next night at my house.

And then I don't know what happened to me. It just burst out. I just blurted out what I really wanted to ask Morgan.

"Morgan, your school records came in while I was working in the office. There must have been a mix-up. You won't believe this. It's actually hilarious. It . . . it said you died five years ago."

Morgan's mouth dropped open.

Had I shocked her?

No. She burst out laughing. She has a low, throaty laugh that seems to come from deep inside her.

She grinned at me. "I thought *everyone* knew that. Yes, it's true. It's so tragic, Julie. I died so young. It wasn't fair. It wasn't fair at all."

15

JULIE CONTINUES

Morgan laughed again. "The report . . . Did it say how I died? Did I have some kind of exotic disease? Or . . . wait . . . Did someone *murder* me?"

For some reason, Zane thought that was a riot and uttered a roar of laughter. "You're a ghost, Morgan," he said, squeezing her arm. "Are you going to haunt us all?"

"The—the letter said it was a car accident," I said.

Morgan nodded. Her smile faded. "Did you say five years ago? And which school were the records from?"

"Five years. And it was Shadyside Middle School."

"Really? Weird. I don't understand the mix-up at all." Her eyes flashed. "I'm glad you were worried about me, Julie."

"We thought maybe you were a zombie," Amber

chimed in. "That would be exciting."

"Well, I *have* been known to eat human flesh," Morgan joked.

Zane turned and made growling noises as he pretended to chew on her shoulder. I noticed a bandage going down Zane's cheek. "What happened to your face?"

He shrugged. "Morgan and I were tossing a Frisbee back and forth. I was telling her about our Ultimate Frisbee games. She threw one too high and fast and—I was such a klutz. I missed it and it cut my cheek."

"You should have seen the blood," Morgan said. "I felt so bad. It was a deep cut." A strange smile crossed her face. She patted Zane's hand. "Zane is a real bleeder."

Zane came over after dinner the next night. He tossed his jacket onto the bench in the entryway, dropped onto the brown leather couch in the den, slipped his backpack to the carpet, and gazed around with those serious, dark raccoon eyes. "Where are your parents?"

"Went to a movie," I said.

Zane used to spend a lot of time at our house. His parents were going through a bad time, and my home was like a safe place for him. He tried to make jokes about his parents' arguments. But I knew him too well. I could see the trouble was tearing him apart.

When they divorced and his father moved away, I think it was kind of a relief for him.

I lowered a basket of tortilla chips and a bowl of salsa onto the coffee table and sat down at the other end of the couch. Sure enough, I heard the *click* of toenails on the wood floor in the hall, and Yancey, our French bulldog came waddling in, wagging his stubby tail.

Yancey adores Zane. For some reason, he likes Zane even better than he likes me.

Yancey barked to be picked up. He's too big a tub to jump on the couch by himself. Zane groaned as he lifted the dog up beside him. Yancey insisted on licking his face. The dog nearly licked the bandage off his cheek.

Yancey finally calmed down and plopped next to Zane, waiting for Zane to start petting his back.

"I should do a comedy bit about Yancey," Zane said, wiping dog drool off his face with one hand. "Maybe like how unsanitary dogs are. And they know it, see. They don't really like to lick people. They are just on a mission to spread germs. Make us all sick. Take over the world."

He lowered his gaze to Yancey. "What do you think? Pretty funny?"

Yancey began panting and put what looked like a grin on his round face.

"Look. He likes it," Zane said. "He's laughing."

I rolled my eyes. "He's a pushover," I said. "He laughs at dust balls on the floor." I took a handful of chips. "Do you have any new ideas?"

"For sure." Zane reached into his backpack and pulled out an iPad. He tapped a few things, then brought the screen to his face. "Uh . . . One idea is about dissecting frogs in biology lab. I mean, why frogs? They've been doing that for a hundred years. Why not make it more interesting, you know? More exciting. Like if the lab teacher brought in a giraffe? Wouldn't that be a lot more exciting, to dissect a giraffe?"

I chewed for a while. I knew he expected me to laugh or at least smile. But I thought it was a terrible idea.

"What else have you got?" I asked.

He squinted at the iPad. "I've been working on this routine about a girlfriend. See, I'll say I have this real bossy girlfriend. She always has to get her way. Then maybe something about how she even tells me when I can go to the bathroom. Like, she has a special hall pass for me at her house. Stuff like that."

You don't have a girlfriend, I thought.

"That's a lot more promising," I said. "We should work up some more bossy-girlfriend jokes." And then, without thinking, I blurted out, "Are you going out with Morgan?"

I could see that my question surprised him. He lowered the iPad to his lap. "No, I'm not. I asked Morgan if she wanted to do something this weekend. I asked her last night at Benson's. And she said she was busy."

Yancey groaned and pressed his body closer against Zane's leg. Zane scratched the back of the dog's ears.

He leaned closer to me. "You know about the bet, right? I mean, Amber heard about it. I'm sure she told you."

I rolled my eyes. "Yes, I know about the bet. You guys are so mature."

"Well, I think Winks won," Zane said. "I think Winks and Morgan are going to be a thing. He—"

"Everyone knows about the bet but Delia," I said. "If it's true, Delia will be heartbroken. You know she's totally in love with Winks."

Zane sighed. He tapped his fingers on the arm of the couch. "Winks says it's over between him and Delia. She just doesn't know it yet."

"You mean he hasn't told her?" I said, raising my voice. "He's breaking up with her, and he hasn't told her?"

"Pretty much," Zane replied. He avoided my gaze, kept his eyes down on Yancey.

"This is bad news," I said. "Delia will be seriously messed up."

Zane didn't reply for a long while. It was so quiet in the room, I could hear the clock ticking on the mantel.

"You guys are ridiculous," I said. "That bet is just . . . juvenile. Not to mention piggish. None of you would be interested in her if she wasn't drop-dead gorgeous."

"You're right," Zane said, still avoiding my eyes. "So what's your point?"

"I don't know," I said. "I don't know what my point is. But—"

"You should tell Delia," he said, finally turning to me. "*You* should do it, Julie. You're Delia's friend."

"No way!" I cried. I jumped to my feet. "Winks has to step up, Zane. You have to talk to Winks and tell him to stop being a baby and just be straight with Delia."

Zane rubbed a hand through his short brown hair. "I don't know . . ."

"You have to do it, Zane," I said. "Delia has to know—uh—"

I stopped because Delia stood in the den doorway.

I blinked, making sure she was really there. Zane made a startled *gulp* sound.

"No one answered the door," she said, "so I just came in. Did I hear someone mention my name?"

I opened my mouth to answer.

"Uh . . . We were just trying to figure out a comedy

routine," Zane said first. "It's about these three girls who make a bet they can be the first to get this guy."

"Sounds very sophisticated," Delia said sarcastically. "Not your kind of thing."

"Oooh." Zane motioned a knife going into his chest. "I think I've just been trolled."

"Has anyone heard from Winks?" Delia asked. "Do you know where he is? I've been trying him all night, and I can't reach him."

16

DEAR DIARY,

Sometimes I wish I was a better writer so that I could completely express what I feel. How to capture the horror and the mystery and the sadness of being dead, yet not? How to capture all my feelings and thoughts about having no heartbeat, but walking among the living?

Yes, it's a heavy secret to keep. And yes, I have to be aware of everything I say, every move I make. It's a secret I can't reveal in any way, or my so-called life with these people will be over.

And then where will I go?

I'm not a ghost. I'm not a zombie. I know what I am. Believe me, I know what I am. I don't like it, but I can't change it. As the expression goes, it is what it is.

So I have no choice. I work harder and harder at hiding my real self and keeping my secret.

And speaking of secrets, Diary, there is one I don't like to think about, but there's no escaping it. One secret that consumes me, that fills me with all kinds of longing.

No, I don't mean that kind of longing. Although, I crave affection like any living human. I crave the warmth of another person, the touch of their skin on my skin. I'm not dead to desire.

But the secret I try to push to the back of my mind is a different kind of longing. It's the hunger I feel when I'm with my new friends. I am hungry all the time I am with them. Hungry as if I were alive.

It's an overwhelming feeling, Diary. And yes, it even makes me dizzy, the intense craving, the growl of my stomach, that driving urge to feed and feed and feed until I am filled with the living blood. Until I am filled with it and the blood is me.

The nectar is so rich and filling. I crave the taste of it, the heaviness of it on my tongue and down my throat. The feel of the red smears of it staining my cheeks and chin.

I could drown in it.

But I've been good, Diary. I've been careful. I've

held myself back, held back my urges, my HUNGER.

These are my new friends. I can't let them know. I can't leave a single hint. But still . . .

I must feed.

And I feel that the time is near. I'm not going to hold back much longer. My craving is too strong.

I'm going to satisfy my hunger before I return to you.

17

WINKS NARRATES

Morgan is HOT. She's so hot, she's on fire. No, that's not enough to describe her hotness. Okay, so I'm not a writer. I don't have a vocabulary to give her full credit for being hot. But take my word, okay?

We were in the front seat of the Camry, going at it pretty well. I mean, we still had our clothes on, but WOW. She was all over the Big Guy.

We held one kiss till I couldn't breathe—and she still didn't want to let go! I mean, I was panting like a dog when I finally pulled my lips from hers.

"You're awesome." I think that's what I managed to say, struggling to catch my breath. I tasted metal, like iron or something. I think my lips were bleeding.

That's how intense Morgan was.

And then her mouth was against mine again, her hands pressing the back of my neck, and she was *licking* the blood off my lips.

Yes, it was a little weird, but it was so sexy. I mean, I felt chills all over. And I was so gone, I mean so into it, I thought I'd explode.

We were parked behind the old Piggly Wiggly that closed last year. No one ever comes back here. We were in our own world. And trust me, it was an awesome world.

I did wonder—only for a few seconds—why this amazing girl picked me. And I did think about Delia, poor little Delia, who is so sweet and quiet and clingy. Delia's face seemed to fade away as I wrapped my arms around Morgan and pulled her closer to me.

Good-bye, Delia. It was nice while it lasted.

But Morgan is major-league awesome.

She didn't shut her eyes when we kissed. Her green eyes locked onto mine. I ran my hand through her copper-colored hair, so smooth and soft.

I uttered a soft gasp as she pulled away suddenly, with a sharp tug of her head. I followed her gaze through the windshield. "Who is that?" Morgan whispered, still holding on to me.

The guy came closer, and I recognized him. Recognized him from his spiky white-blond hair and the weird blank eyes.

Cal.

Delia's stepbrother.

"It's . . . Cal," I murmured.

Morgan squeezed my arm. "Do you know him?"

I didn't answer. I saw that he had a baseball bat in one hand. He began swinging it as he came close.

"Hey—!" I shouted. I rolled down the window. "Hey—!"

He pointed at me with his free hand. "Didn't I warn you?" he shouted.

"Warn me? Stop." I grabbed the handle and shoved open the car door. "Hey—stop. What are you going to do?"

He raised the bat in both hands.

"Stop!" I screamed. "Are you crazy?"

He got this fierce look on his face as he swung the bat down hard on the trunk of the car.

It made a sick, cracking sound as the metal caved in under the smash of the bat.

A deep shudder ran down my back, as if *I* had been hit.

"Are you crazy? Are you *crazy*?" I shrieked.

Cal scowled at me, the silvery eyes narrowed. He didn't say a word.

He raised the bat again and came at me.

"Winks—*do* something! Stop him!" I heard Morgan's scream from inside the car. "Stop him. He's going to *kill* us!"

18

WINKS CONTINUES THE STORY

I froze in panic for a moment.

Cal stood gaping at me with the bat poised.

I sucked in a deep breath, struggled to slow my racing heartbeats—and dove back into the car.

He took a few strides along the side of the car. Was he going to smash my window?

I fumbled with the key, finally turned the ignition, and slammed my foot on the gas. The car heaved forward, sending Morgan and me back against the seat with a hard jerk. We squealed away. It sounded like something in a Fast and Furious movie.

I raised my eyes to the rearview mirror. And saw Cal standing there, watching us roar away, his bat still raised in front of him.

"That was *horrible*!" Morgan cried, holding on to my arm. "He wrecked your car. Who was that?"

I didn't want to tell her that Cal was Delia's stepbrother. I didn't reply.

"No. Really," Morgan insisted. "Do you know him, Winks? He sure seemed to know you."

I shook my head. "I think he's just some crazy guy. I mean, maybe he escaped from a hospital or something. We should call the police."

She narrowed her eyes at me. "But . . . he said, 'Didn't I warn you?' You must have seen him before."

I swung the car onto Division Street. "No. Never. I'd remember someone like him, you know."

"But why—"

"Beats me." I groaned. "My mom is going to kill me about the smashed trunk. She loves this car like it's another kid."

Morgan crossed her arms in front of her and stared straight ahead through the windshield. The afternoon sun was lowering behind the trees, and long shadows rolled over the car as we drove. "I'm . . . still shaking," she said, hugging herself.

"Me too," I confessed. "An insane nut like that can do anything. I guess we were lucky.

"Hey, where am I dropping you?" I asked, trying to

change the subject. "I don't know where you live."

She pointed. "You can drop me at that corner. I promised I'd see a friend."

I pulled to the corner. She leaned forward and gave me a quick peck on the cheek. "Well . . . it's been *exciting*," she said. And she slid out of the car.

I watched her stride along the sidewalk. She has such a sexy walk. I wanted to run after her and grab her and start all over again. Crazy. I know. It was like I was hypnotized or something.

She turned a corner, and I quickly snapped out of it. And remembered Cal and the baseball bat and how he wrecked my mom's car and threatened me.

Didn't I warn you? That's what he'd said. Like he was the law or something. How could shy, quiet Delia have such an insane, out-of-his-mind stepbrother?

"No more," I murmured to myself. "Delia has got to call off Cal. She has got to talk to him. He's totally deranged."

I squealed into a sharp U-turn and headed toward Delia's house.

Her brother, Duke, opened the front door. He's a strange dude, very lanky with long tangles of hay-colored hair. His clothes kind of hang on him. His sleeves are too long. He always makes me think of a scarecrow.

Duke is ten years older than Delia. I've never really talked with him. He has a quiet voice that dribbles down his stubbly chin. I can never hear half of what he says.

"Is Delia home?"

He nodded and stepped back so I could enter the front hall. The entryway was dark, except for red evening sunlight slanting through a wide living room window. The walls were bare. No paintings or artwork of any kind.

I heard classical music playing from the back of the house. It was deep and creepy, low organ music, like from a horror movie.

Duke had a shuffling walk. His shoes scraped the floor noisily. He nodded his head with each step. He gestured with one hand into the living room.

Delia sat on a small gray couch, her back to me. She was reading a book on a Kindle. Her ringlets of dark hair shone in the light from the screen.

She turned and uttered a surprised cry as I appeared. Her smile spread over her pale, pretty face. "Winks? What a nice surprise."

She closed the Kindle cover and patted the couch cushion beside her. "Don't just stand there. Come here."

I came around to the front of the couch and dropped

down beside her. I opened my mouth to talk, but she threw her arms around me and pulled me close and started kissing me.

She made loud breathing sounds as she kissed me, her eyes closed. She's kind of passionate, I guess. I mean, I know she's very emotional.

She wore a tight pale blue sweater over white tennis shorts. Her whole body was so light and thin, like a delicate bird. I always felt like a big elephant next to her. Seriously. I was afraid I might go to hug her and *crush* her.

I pulled back. "Listen, Delia, we have to talk."

Her dark eyes went wide. She studied my face, as if trying to read what was on my mind. "Winks—your lip is bleeding," she said. She touched my mouth gently with one hand. "Your lips . . . they're swollen. Are you okay?"

From kissing Morgan, I realized. *It was so intense . . .*

"I . . . uh . . . guess they're just dry," I said.

She started to stand up. "I can get you some Chap-Stick."

I grabbed her arm and pulled her back down beside me. "No. Listen. I have to talk to you, Delia."

She tugged at a ringlet of hair that had become tangled. Her eyes were locked on mine.

"You have got to tell Cal to lay off," I said. "Your

crazy stepbrother is following me everywhere. He's out of control, Delia. He's totally wacked out. And he's dangerous."

She shut her eyes for a moment, breaking the connection between us. Her face twisted in confusion. "Excuse me? What are you talking about, Winks?"

"I'm talking about Cal. Your psycho stepbrother."

She grabbed my arm. "Are you totally losing it? I don't have a stepbrother."

PART THREE

19

LIAM NARRATES

"The Phillips screwdriver? Is that the pointy one?" Zane asked. He rummaged around in the toolbox on the floor of my garage.

I nodded. "Yeah. The pointy one." I set the drone engine down beside the frame.

"I can't find it," Zane said, turning to me.

I rolled my eyes. I walked over and picked up the Phillips screwdriver. It was right on top. "You know, it's a good thing you're funny, Zane. Or else you'd be useless."

Zane snickered. "Nicest thing you ever said about me."

I pushed him out of my way. "It wasn't a compliment. Can you at least read the instructions? Do we install the camera first or the engine first?"

Zane scratched his dark hair. "Where *are* the instructions?"

"Are you joking? They're in your shirt pocket," I said.

He pulled out the instruction sheet and unfolded it. "I can't read it. It's upside down," he said.

He laughed at his own joke.

This drone was taking forever to put together. And it came out of a kit, so it shouldn't have taken much time at all. But my two helpers—Zane and Winks—weren't exactly mechanical geniuses. Shoelaces were almost too complicated for them. They both wore Velcro. Seriously.

It was getting dark. The afternoon sun was fading. One of the ceiling lights in the garage was out, and a dark shadow spread over us. I knew Mom would be calling me in for dinner soon.

Zane's eyes ran down the page of instructions. "Camera comes before motor," he said. He raised his gaze to me. "Do you really think this is going to work? You'll be taking pictures from this thing?"

"Video," I said. "It's a video camera. It's going to be totally cool. Let me see the diagram. I'm not sure where the camera gets installed." I reached for the sheet of paper.

"Is this legal?" Zane asked.

I squinted at him. "Legal? Is *what* legal?"

"Flying your own drone. Don't you need a permit or something?"

"You mean like a driver's license?" I shrugged. "I don't know."

"If everyone had a drone, there'd be a thousand crashes a day," Zane said.

"Probably," I replied. "I don't know. I didn't look it up. My uncle Bill sent this to me, so it must be okay."

"But what if—"

I clapped my hand over Zane's mouth. "Stop asking questions. You're not helping me. If you just ask me a bunch of questions, we'll never be able to fly this thing."

He tried to bite my hand. I swiped it away and turned from him. I studied the instruction sheet.

"Hey, look. A squirrel," Zane said. He pointed out the open garage door.

A fat brown squirrel stood on its hind legs on the edge of the driveway. "So what?" I said. "Haven't you seen a squirrel before?"

Zane's eyes flashed. "Do you know why a squirrel hides his nuts?"

I groaned. "Zane—you've told me that joke a hundred times. And I laughed the first fifty times. Do you think you could give it a rest?"

He laughed. "Maybe I have a new punch line."

"No. You don't," I said. "Even if you do, I don't want to hear it."

I studied the drone-parts chart. The brushless motor fit into a motor mount near the back. I dug in the box till I found the parts to the motor mount.

Zane's phone beeped. He pulled it out and stared at the screen. "A text from Julie."

"Does she want to come be my helper?" I asked. "She'd be better than you." I shook my head. "*Anyone* would be better."

Zane sighed. He stared thoughtfully at the phone screen. "She's giving me a hard time," he murmured. He ran a hand tensely through his dark hair.

I lowered the motor-mount parts to the floor. "About what?"

"About Winks," Zane said. He kept his eyes on his phone. Like he was embarrassed to face me or something.

I snickered. "What did Winks do? Act like Winks?"

Zane slid the phone into his pocket. "She wants me to talk to him. She wants me to tell him he isn't being fair to Delia. He has to be honest with her."

I couldn't keep the surprise off my face. "Julie wants you to have a serious heart-to-heart with Winks? Isn't that *girls'* stuff?"

Zane didn't laugh. He sighed again. "Julie thinks Delia is going to get hurt. You know how she is."

"Yeah. Crazy."

"Crazy about Winks," Zane said. "Seriously. She's so into him, it's unreal. Like she thinks they're going to get married or something."

"She's only known him a couple of months," I said.

"That doesn't matter," Zane said. "Julie thinks—"

"Winks should stick with Delia," I told him, "and leave Morgan for you and me." I laughed, but he didn't. For a comedian, he was always serious.

"I have to talk to him," Zane said. "I promised Julie."

"And tell him *what*?"

"If he doesn't care about Delia, he should tell her. You know. Break up with her."

I shook my head. "Winks will just laugh and probably gut-punch you. He won't even answer you. That's the way he rolls. You know that."

Zane pulled out his phone again. "I'm going to call Winks right now. Julie will just stay in my face till I do it."

I rolled my eyes again. "I'll just clean up. Thanks for all your help. I sure get a lot done when you're around. Maybe you could come tomorrow and we could stare at the instruction sheet again all afternoon."

"Do you know what they say about sarcasm?" Zane asked.

"No. What do they say?"

"Gee," he said in a smarmy voice, "I don't know. Why don't you tell me?"

"LOL," I said. "LOL, Zane. Remind me to laugh later."

I picked up the motor-mount parts and dropped them back into the box. Then I started to shove tools back into the toolbox.

Zane leaned against the garage wall and phoned Winks. I clanked some wrenches together and tried to make a racket so he couldn't hear well. He deserved it. He didn't even try to be helpful.

He waved at me to be quiet, but I didn't stop.

"Listen, Winks, can you hear me?" he shouted into the phone. "Want to hang out tomorrow night? You know. The weekend starts on Thursday, right?"

I heard Winks's reply. For some reason, Zane had put his phone on speaker. Maybe he thought he could hear better that way.

"I can't," Winks told him. "I babysit for my cousin Spencer every Thursday night."

"Oh, right." Zane thought for a moment. "Well, maybe I could stop by?"

"Not a good idea," Winks said. "My aunt and uncle are totally tense people. They won't want me having guests. It's like they start shaking if a fly gets into the house."

"What are you saying, Winks? That I'm like an insect?"

"No. I just mean they don't like surprises," Winks replied. "It would freak them out. Seriously."

"Okay, okay," Zane said. "Catch you later." Then he added, "Hey, have you seen Morgan?"

"In my dreams," Winks replied.

Zane clicked off. He frowned at the phone, then slid it back into his pocket.

"Guess your heart-to-heart will have to wait," I said.

"How did *I* get to be the guy, anyway?" Zane grumbled.

"You just are. You're the dude," I said. "I know you'll get Winks straightened out. He's—"

But my thought was cut short when I saw something in the garage window.

A face. A guy's face. Staring in. A guy with spiked white-blond hair and weird silvery eyes.

"Hey—!" I shouted.

Zane spun around. He saw the guy, too. Zane uttered a startled cry.

The weird eyes gazed in at us.

Zane and I froze for a moment. I shouted again. "Hey—who *are* you?"

He stared. Then we both took off. Our sneakers slapped the concrete floor as we bolted out of the garage. Then we spun to the side.

"Hey—come back!" we screamed.

The guy ran full-speed to the back of the yard, leaning forward as he ran, his arms swinging. Zane and I watched him hurtle over the wooden fence.

"Come back! Hey—!"

We were breathing hard as we reached the fence. I hoisted myself up and searched in both directions.

Gone. The guy had vanished.

20

WINKS CONTINUES THE STORY

Four-year-olds have a lot of energy, especially around bedtime. Spencer is a great kid. But I can never get him to bed before nine. I lie and tell his parents he was asleep by seven thirty, otherwise they'd freak out.

He has wavy brown hair and big gray-blue eyes, pink cheeks I like to pinch, and a goofy smile that shows a lot of square little baby teeth. He's tall for his age. At least, that's what my aunt and uncle tell me. I mean, I can't tell. Spencer is the only four-year-old I know.

I guess he's tall. I *know* he's strong. He likes to punch me in the stomach, and I really feel it. He likes to climb on me, too. It's like he thinks I'm a mountain or something. We have a lot of wrestling matches that end up with me on my back on the floor, helpless beneath him.

Yes, I always let him win.

But at nine o'clock I've got homework to do. And I've got Delia texting me every five minutes. I *told* her I was babysitting. She knows I babysit for Spencer every Thursday night. So why doesn't she give me a break?

I was sitting in the middle of the couch with a pile of picture books on the coffee table in front of me. Spencer was climbing me, messing up my hair, poking a finger in my nose. He thinks he's a riot, and I kind of agree.

"Be a robot," he said. "Winks, go ahead. Robot. Do the robot."

He likes when I stagger around the living room stiff-legged and move like a robot. Then he imitates me, and we both do a robot dance until we fall down laughing.

"No robot. Too late for the robot," I said. I patted the couch cushion beside me. "Sit down. It's bedtime. Let's read a bedtime book."

"No books!" he cried. "No books." He swung his arm and knocked the pile of books off the coffee table. "Do the robot."

I ignored him and picked up a book from the floor. "Here's a good one. Let's read it," I said. "Come on, Spencer. Time to read a book."

He eyed it like it was a bowl of spinach. "I don't like

that book." He crossed his skinny arms in front of him.

"Yes, you do. I read it to you last week. *Frog and Toad*, remember? You made me read it three times?"

"Well, I'm tired of it. What's the difference between a frog and a toad anyway?"

"I don't know," I said. I patted the cushion again. "Let's read the book and find out."

"No. No books," Spencer growled. "Can I have a cookie?"

I brought my face close to his. "Will you go to bed if I give you a cookie?"

"Two cookies," he said with a straight face.

"And you'll go to bed?"

"And a juice box. And two books."

Spencer could be a four-year-old lawyer. He's a great negotiator.

I talked him down to a cookie, some juice, and *Frog and Toad*. And he was asleep almost before his head hit the pillow.

I wished I could spend more time with *Frog and Toad*, but I had *A Tale of Two Cities* to read, and I was two chapters behind the rest of the class. That called for a lot of faking it during class discussions. Luckily, I'm seriously good at faking it.

I was fumbling through the book, trying to find my place, when my phone chimed. Of course, it was a text from Delia:

R u still there? Want to come over when u r done?

I started to reply—when the doorbell rang. The sound startled me. I'd never heard it before. I was always alone with Spencer on Thursday nights.

I closed my book and climbed to my feet. *Zane*, I realized. *I told Zane not to come, but he showed up anyway.*

I crossed to the front entryway and pulled open the front door. "Listen, Zane—" I started.

But then I stopped and let out a little cry of surprise. "Hey, what are *you* doing here?"

21

WINKS CONTINUES

A pleased smile spread over Morgan's lips. Under the porch light, her coppery hair glowed as if on fire. She squeezed my hand. "Are you surprised?"

"Well . . . yeah." Surprised wasn't the word. I could feel my heart beating fast in my chest. I couldn't stop staring at her face in the bright circle of light, like a spotlight.

She laughed. "Aren't you going to let me in?"

I realized I was blocking the door, just standing there like some kind of water buffalo, frozen by those jewel-like green eyes. "Hey, come in." I managed to back out of her way.

She followed me into the living room. "Lots of toys. Looks like you were having fun," she said. She stepped over a Lego castle Spencer and I had built.

"He doesn't understand about cleaning up afterward," I said. "It's just not a concept to him."

"Or you either," she joked, gazing around the cluttered mess of blocks and toys and puzzles.

I sat on one edge of the couch and slid a bunch of books onto the floor so she could join me. She settled closer than I'd imagined. She wore a soft-looking pale green sweater over jeans shredded at the knees.

She clasped her hands in her lap, and for the first time, I noticed that she had a tiny tattoo on the back of each hand. A blue bird with its wings spread. How had I missed those before?

"How did you find me?" I asked.

She took my hand. Her eyes locked on mine. "I have my ways," she said, lowering her voice to a whisper.

"No. Really," I said. "Who told you I'd be here?"

She held on to my hand. "No one." She flashed me a teasing smile. "I wanted to find you, so I did."

That didn't make any sense, but why should I care?

She leaned her head so that a wave of her soft hair brushed my face. It sent a tingling feeling to the back of my neck.

She brought her lips to my ear and whispered, "I was lonely. Do you ever feel lonely?"

Before I had a chance to answer, we were kissing.

She placed her hands around my neck and pulled my face close, and we kissed, gently at first, but then harder. And we held it . . . held it for a long time, until I was breathless.

I started to pull my head back and break the kiss. But her mouth was insistent, not retreating, and she tightened her grip on my neck and held me in place.

Yes, it was exciting. This beautiful girl who was so into me and so eager to be close. But at the same time, I wondered why she was so desperate to be in control.

And then as we caught our breath, she pressed her cheek against mine. Her skin was surprisingly cold despite the heat in the room. I raised my eyes to the clock on the mantel. Almost nine thirty.

A ripple of panic ran down my back. I had to get Morgan out of the house before my aunt and uncle returned.

She slid her forehead against mine. She licked my ear. Then she pressed her lips hard against mine, and we started another long kiss.

I wrapped my arms around her waist. I'd never felt anything like this. She was so intense . . . so *hungry*.

Where was this going?

I couldn't help it. I glanced at the clock again. I imagined my aunt and uncle's car rolling up the gravel driveway. I didn't want this to end. But . . .

I could feel panic mixing with my excitement.

And then Morgan pulled her head back. She had her arms around my shoulders. Her lips were swollen, and her green eyes were half closed. "Listen . . . ," she whispered.

I couldn't reply. I was struggling to catch my breath.

"I'm going to be honest with you, honey," she said, trailing a fingernail lightly down my cheek. "I'm going to open up to you—because you're my honey."

"What do you mean?" I managed to choke out.

She didn't answer. She pulled me back to her and kissed me, really hard this time, so hard I could feel her teeth, so hard it hurt.

I tried to pull back. But her eyes were shut tight and her arms had me clamped against her.

And as I stared into her face, she began to change. At first, I thought I was imagining it. But then I realized it was really happening.

Her creamy skin sagged. Like her cheeks were melting. And her pale skin darkened to a dark yellow-green.

I blinked a few times. No. This wasn't happening. My eyes were going crazy. Something had happened to me, making me see things.

What was that sour smell? Like a damp, moldy basement? Where had it suddenly come from?

I tried harder to free myself from her grip. But her teeth were digging into my lips now. And her eyes . . . those beautiful eyes . . . her eyes sank deep into their sockets.

As I gaped in horror, her lips brushed mine. Loose, floppy lips, the color of raw liver. "Come on, honey," she whispered in a harsh, raspy voice that made my skin crawl. "Don't you see how much I need you?"

I started to choke. The horror of it. Seeing her so ugly, like some kind of creature, all shriveled and shrunk and eyeless with her skin oozing wet down her face.

I tried to escape. But she held me with inhuman strength.

"Please—" I gasped. "Please—"

She held me tight and began to bite me. She bit my cheek. Bit my mouth. Sharp teeth that felt pointed. Bit my cheek again, frantic biting now, faster, harder.

"Please—"

The teeth puncturing my skin, sending currents of pain down my whole body. Another bite. Another slashing bite. Cutting away at my cheeks, my lips . . . and then my neck.

22

WINKS NARRATES

A howl of pain escaped my throat. I shoved her hard with both hands. It caused her to loosen her grip, and I tossed my body forward. I hurtled to the floor on my hands and knees.

Blood from my face and neck trickled onto my shirt. I tried to raise myself to my feet, but I suddenly felt too dizzy. The room was spinning. The ugly creature on the couch appeared to tilt one way, then the other.

Too unsteady to run, I forced myself into a sitting position. Then I shut my eyes and raised my hands over my face as if protecting myself.

"Come back, honey," the creature growled. Her voice was low and pleading, from somewhere deep in her throat. "You know you are my honey, don't you?"

"Who . . . who *are* you?" I screamed. "*What* are you? What do you want?"

"You don't have to shout, honey," she rasped. I opened my eyes and gazed up at her. Her eye sockets were black holes. Her teeth poked out over her swollen mouth.

"I need you," she said. "I can't look pretty again without you."

"What do you mean?" I shrieked. "What are you *talking* about? You—you're a *monster*!"

"Don't hurt my feelings," she said. "You know you want to be my honey." And then she tossed back her hideous head and uttered a booming, ugly laugh, a laugh that made her belly bounce up and down beneath her sweater.

I turned my head and eyed the door. Could I get out of there before she grabbed me? And what about Spencer? I couldn't leave him here with a—a monster in the house.

"What do you *want*?" I cried.

"Honey, I *said* I'd tell you the truth. I said I'd be open with you. Why do you doubt me?"

I didn't know how to answer that question.

"You want me to be pretty again, don't you?" she rasped.

I couldn't answer that question, either. "Who are you *really*?" I demanded.

She rolled the lips between her fingers. "I'm Morgan. Just Morgan. Morgan Fear," she said.

I swallowed. "Morgan Fear? But you told everyone—"

"I took another girl's name. The other Morgan in my class. I took her name. Morgan Marks died, too. She died like me."

Am I dreaming this?

My brain was spinning. I knew the story of the Fear family, their long history of horror, their knowledge of the dark arts, and the curse that doomed them—to evil and horror for all eternity.

"You . . . you *died*?" I stammered.

She nodded her ugly head. "But I'm a Fear. I know how to deal with things like *death*." Again, she tossed back her head and roared with cold, ugly laughter.

"Please—let me go," I said, my voice catching in my throat. "Let me take Spencer and go. I won't tell anyone about this. I promise."

Outside the window, I heard a car rumble past. Were my aunt and uncle back? No. Just a passing car.

"I promise," I repeated. "I won't tell anyone. Just let Spencer and me go."

She shook her eyeless head. "I can't. I can't let you go, Winks. I need you. You're my honey—"

"No!" I screamed. "No! Please—"

"I need my honey," she growled. "You have no idea how much I need my honey."

I suddenly realized I was still seated on the floor. My legs shaking, I climbed to my knees. Fighting off my dizziness, I glanced at the front door again. Could I stand up and make it out of here before she stopped me?

"I must stay alive," she rasped. "I must stay beautiful. And how can I do that without you?"

"Me?" I choked out. "Why do you need *me*?"

"Isn't it obvious? I need you, Winks," she said, "because I need to *feed*."

And before I could move, she was on me.

She shot off the couch and dove on top of me. She shoved hard, pushed me over, onto my back. I landed hard. I felt the breath whoosh out of me in a painful rush.

She sat on top of me. Straddled me. Pressed both of my arms against the carpet.

Then she leaned down. Brought her face to my throat.

I screamed as her teeth dug deep into my throat.

I screamed again as she began to drink.

23

WINKS CONTINUES

I struggled and squirmed. But she sat heavily on top of me, pinning my arms down. No way I could kick her or roll out from under her.

I felt hot liquid on my throat. My blood. And I could hear a lapping sound, and sometimes what sounded like a slurp, and hungry swallowing.

I shook my head from side to side, trying to avoid the pain of her needle teeth.

"Hold still!" Morgan shouted. "I don't want a shake—I want a smoothie."

I felt a harsh scraping on my neck and knew it was her tongue licking up my blood. She lowered her head and drank hungrily, as if she had been starving.

The slurping sounds rang in my ears, then seemed far away . . . far away . . . like ocean waves in the distance.

I knew I was getting weak. *She is draining me.*

I don't have much time left. If I don't act now . . .

I took in a deep breath. Then I swung my body hard to the left, swung with all my remaining strength. I jerked an arm free. Her hand slid off as I pulled the arm up.

And I punched her as hard as I could in the face.

It felt like hitting solid stone.

She made a gurgling sound and toppled off me, landing on her side. It gave me just enough time to swing around, roll to my knees, lurch to my feet.

My throat ached. I could feel the warm blood trickling down my neck. My legs didn't want to cooperate. But I forced them forward. I took a few staggering steps toward the front door.

Behind me, I glimpsed Morgan shake off the pain from my punch. She rose up with an animal growl. Dove forward, grabbing for me with both hands.

"Come back, honey. I need to finish."

"N-no," I stammered. Just a few feet from the front door. But I felt so weak, my legs so rubbery and heavy, as if they weighed a thousand pounds.

And she was charging after me now, growling, curling and uncurling her hands like claws as she tore across the room.

I can't make it.

I struggled to breathe. Struggled to move.

She roared closer, running hard. I spun around in time to see her stumble over a stack of Spencer's puzzles. The puzzles flew in all directions as she went down.

Morgan's arms flew up as she crashed to the floor. She uttered a loud gasp as her head smacked against it. Her head hit hard once, then bounced and hit again.

Was she out? She wasn't moving.

I grabbed the front doorknob with a trembling hand. I pulled the door open, almost hitting myself with it, and stumbled onto the front stoop.

The feel of the fresh night air was overwhelming. I suddenly felt as if my lungs would burst. I felt the stain of blood on my neck, still warm.

I turned and slammed the front door shut. My car shone under a streetlamp at the curb beyond the front yard.

Got to get away. Got to get away.

My shoes scraped and crunched down the gravel driveway. The only other sounds were the wheezing of my breath and the bass-drum pounding of my heart.

I was halfway down the driveway, but my car still seemed a mile away.

The last thing I heard was Spencer's high voice, ringing out from the house. "Winks? Winks? Are you okay?"

24

JULIE NARRATES

I was driving Delia home from Amber's house. I had to click the radio off because Delia was talking so quietly, and even though she was sitting in the passenger seat right next to me in my mom's tiny Civic, I had trouble hearing her.

"You're in a weird mood," I said, slowing for a stop sign, then turning right onto Harvest Street. It was late and there were few cars.

Why do I have to live in a town that shuts down at eight o'clock?

Delia said something in reply. But the words seemed to dribble down her chin, and I couldn't hear them.

She kept her eyes straight ahead, staring out the windshield. I saw that her phone was gripped tightly in her hand. Her other hand teased a ringlet of her dark hair.

"First you came late," I said. "And then you barely said a word. Didn't you like Amber's new puppy? I thought he was adorable. And he certainly had a thing for you."

Delia frowned. "I couldn't get him off my leg."

I laughed. "That's what I meant."

"What kind of dog *is* that?" Delia asked.

"It's half Cavalier and half poodle. That's what Amber said. It's called a Cavapoo."

"Disgusting name," Delia muttered. "Couldn't they think of something better?"

"What's your problem tonight?" I demanded. Of course, I knew her problem had to be Winks. What other problem could she have? "How come you were so late getting to Amber's?"

She was silent for a long moment. "I was trying to reach Winks," she said finally. She rolled the phone in her hand. "He didn't answer any of my texts."

"Well, it's Thursday night," I said. I slowed for a red light. "You know he babysits his cousin on Thursday."

"I know," Delia said. "But he always answers my texts. And he always calls me when Spencer goes to sleep."

I knew what was going on. That pig Winks was trying to show Delia that he really didn't care much about her anymore. Instead of being straight with her, he was being a big baby and letting her hang in the wind.

An SUV with its brights on moved toward us. I was blinded by the light for a moment, so I hit the brake and waited for the SUV to pass.

"Delia, you're not really worried about Winks, are you?" I asked. I still had the white circles of light in my eyes.

She twisted the phone in her hand. "Well, actually, yes. I don't understand—"

"If you're really worried," I said, "let's stop at his aunt's house."

She blinked. "Really?"

"Why not? I've known Marie and Art for a long time," I said. "Winks's uncle Art worked with my dad for a while before he started his own IT company."

I made a right and headed into the Valley Acres section of Linden, where Art and Marie lived. Valley Acres is the rich part of town, and they have a big house with a pool and a three-car garage, and a glass greenhouse in the back where they grow orchids.

A few minutes later, I reached the house and pulled to the curb behind another car parked there. It took me a few seconds to recognize Winks's mother's Camry. "His car is still here," I said.

Delia hesitated. She ran a hand through her hair, pushing the ringlets into place. She peered up at the house. "Weird. Why are all the lights on?"

I climbed out of the car. The air was cool and smelled like pine. I stretched my arms above my head. Delia was right. It appeared that every light in the house was on.

We crunched our way up the gravel drive. I heard voices from the back of the house. Art and Marie were shouting. I heard Spencer's voice, too. Why was he up so late?

I knocked on the kitchen door, and Winks's uncle Art pulled it open immediately. His blond hair was standing up, pushed to one side, as if it had been blown by the wind. His eyes were watery and wide, and his cheeks were bright red. "Julie? Have you seen Winks?" he demanded without saying hello or anything.

"Huh?" The question took me by surprise. I heard Delia gasp behind me.

I stepped into the house. Marie stood at the hallway door. She still had her denim jacket on. I guessed they had just returned home. She had her hands clenched down at her sides. Her expression was angry.

"This is Delia," I said, motioning toward her.

Delia offered an awkward hello. But Winks's aunt and uncle didn't seem to hear it or even to see her.

"Where is Winks?" Art repeated, his eyes questioning me, kind of pleading.

"Do you girls know?" Marie said in a harsh whisper. "He left Spencer all alone. When Art and I got home, the front door was wide-open. And no sign of Winks. We were terrified."

"Thank God Spencer is okay," Art said. "When we saw the front door open like that, and the blood by the couch, we . . . we . . . didn't know *what* to think."

I walked over to the couch. There was the tiniest trickle of blood staining the white carpet. It might have been evidence of a paper cut, but not much more.

"This is crazy," I said. "Winks would never leave Spencer."

"Yes, he did!" Spencer cried. He stepped out from behind his hiding place, his mother. He was in a pair of *Star Wars* pajamas. "I shouted for Winks. But he was gone."

"I've been texting him," Delia said in a tiny voice, holding up her phone as if for evidence. "But he never answered."

Marie gritted her teeth. She jammed her hands into her jacket pockets. "I don't believe this. I really don't.

How could he be so irresponsible?"

"Wait a minute," I said. "His car is still here." I motioned toward the front of the house. "It's still at the curb. He wouldn't leave without his car."

Art shook his head. He grabbed the back of a kitchen stool, as if he needed support to hold himself up. "It doesn't make sense. He has never left before."

Spencer tugged at the front of his pajama shirt. "A girl came," he told his mother.

Marie blinked. "A girl?"

Spencer nodded. "A girl came and they had a fight."

Marie hunched down and brought her face close to Spencer's. "A girl? Are you sure?"

"Yes. They had a fight. Then they left."

"You heard that from your room?" Art asked him.

Spencer hesitated. "Maybe I peeked a little."

"You saw the girl?" Delia demanded. "What did she look like?"

Spencer thought about it. "I don't remember."

"What color hair did she have?" Delia asked him.

He thought again. "I don't remember."

I could see that Delia was desperate to know who visited Winks. But Spencer wasn't being very helpful.

"Maybe I didn't see her," he admitted. "Maybe I only heared her."

"It just doesn't make sense," I said again. "You know that Winks is crazy about Spencer. He loves coming here every week. He told me. So . . . he wouldn't just run away with some girl. And leave his car behind."

"Then how do you explain it?" Marie asked, her voice cracking with emotion.

Delia raised her phone. "I'll try calling him again."

We all stared as she punched Winks's number. After a few seconds, she lowered the phone from her ear and sighed. "It went right to voice mail."

"I tried calling his mother," Art said. "First thing I did when I couldn't find him. I woke her up. She didn't have a clue."

"Probably too trashed to even recognize Winks," Marie muttered.

"Marie!" Art snapped. "Don't talk like that in front of Spencer."

"Don't tell me how to talk," Marie shot back.

Spencer laughed. "Too trashed."

Art placed a hand on his shoulder. "Don't say that, Spencer."

"Too trashed?" He laughed. "Too trashed? What does *that* mean?"

"Let's get you back in bed," Art said, giving Spencer a little push toward the door.

"No. I want to see Winks."

Art and Spencer started arguing about getting Spencer to bed.

"Maybe we should call the police," Delia said. "Maybe something has happened to Winks."

"He left with a girl," Marie said. "That's what happened."

"But he wouldn't leave his car," I insisted. I started toward the kitchen door. "Maybe he and the girl went outside for a moment to talk. Maybe he's nearby."

Delia grabbed my arm. "What girl?" she whispered. "Who was it?"

"How should I know?" I snapped. Of course, I knew it had to be Morgan Marks. But why get Delia even more upset?

Did Winks really leave with her? I wondered. Sure, she's hot and everything. And sure, Winks is an idiot when it comes to a seriously pretty girl.

But even Winks couldn't be so irresponsible to abandon his cousin on an impulse, just to be with Morgan.

Maybe he and Morgan stepped outside so they wouldn't wake Spencer up, I thought. But he wouldn't leave the front door wide-open. And they both would have seen Art and Marie's car pull up the driveway.

It didn't make sense. My head was spinning and my

cheeks were burning hot, even in the cool night air. A bright half-moon made everything appear silvery and unreal. The shrubs, the lawn, the trees all shimmered, as if in a dream.

Delia and I made our way down the driveway, our shoes crunching on the gravel, along the tall hedge that separates Art and Marie's yard from their neighbors.

Without thinking, we both began to shout Winks's name. Our voices rang out through the silent night. A dog began barking somewhere down the block. But no reply from Winks.

We were near the street when Delia stopped suddenly. She grabbed my wrist tightly. "Is that . . . ? Is that . . . ?"

I followed her gaze. At first, I thought someone had piled some shoes and old clothes at the bottom of the hedge. But then I saw an arm. And the figure sprawled on his side in the grass beside the hedge came into focus.

Delia lurched across the driveway and dropped down beside him. "Winks? Winks? *Winks?*" Her shouts rose until they became a frightened shriek.

She grabbed his shoulder with both hands. She shook him hard.

My breath caught in my throat. I wanted to join her but my legs wouldn't cooperate.

"Winks? Winks? *Winks?*"

Still holding on to his shoulder with both hands, Delia turned to me. "He's dead. He's dead, Julie," she cried. "Winks is dead."

25

JULIE CONTINUES THE STORY

One hour later. We were all still there, tense, horrified, not believing what was happening. To me, everything seemed unreal. The lights were too bright. Everyone was talking too fast and moved as if on fast-forward. Nothing was at the right speed.

And my thoughts couldn't keep up with what I knew to be true.

Winks was dead. My friend. A guy I had known most of my life. Dead. I would never see him again, never laugh at one of his crazy schemes or stupid jokes. Never see his goofy smile or hear him laugh.

Delia was crying hysterically. I knew I should take her home, but she refused to leave. I stayed with her, hugging her, holding her when her crying started to make her whole body shake.

Winks's mom huddled with Art and Marie. She had a stunned look on her face, her eyes glassy, kept in a gaze at the floor. Marie brought her a cup of tea, but she asked for bourbon.

Winks's dad lives in Kansas City. I didn't know if he had been called yet or not. "It's like a bad dream," Mrs. Winkleman kept repeating. "A bad dream and I'm going to wake up. Rich can't be gone. I know I'll wake up." She asked Marie for another glass of bourbon.

Art had somehow gotten Spencer to bed. Despite the tension of the night, the little guy had been yawning his head off, and he didn't put up much of a fight when Art picked him up and carried him to his bedroom.

There were Linden police officers everywhere. At first, they had demanded we all leave the crime area. But then one of their officers said we could stay. "The crime scene is already polluted," he told two other uniformed cops.

I hugged Delia and asked her for the tenth time if she'd like me to drive her home. She was hesitating, wiping her eyes, then crying some more, and I think she was deciding that it was time to leave.

But a serious-looking gray-haired man in a long blue overcoat, despite the warm spring weather, strode across the living room and stopped in front of Winks's mom and Art and Marie.

"I'm the medical examiner," he announced. "Anderson."

Two cops, one in uniform, one plainclothes, stepped up to hear what he had to report. He turned away from Winks's mom and gave his findings to them.

"He's been dead about two hours, give or take. I found bruises on his neck. And then something strange." Anderson glanced at Winks's mom. I could see he was deciding whether to tell the next part in front of her. "I'm so sorry for your loss," he said. I guess he realized he had been all business and kind of cold.

He turned back to the officers. "I found something strange. Cuts on the face. And two sets of puncture marks on the throat."

The plainclothes officer, an older man, nearly bald, pale with faded gray eyes and a sad hound-dog expression, tapped the medical examiner on the arm. "Two puncture marks or two *sets* of puncture marks, Sid?"

"Two sets."

The uniformed officer spoke in a whisper. But I could still hear him across the room. "You mean like in a vampire movie?"

Anderson shrugged. "His throat was definitely bitten. But even in the shaky light from my halogen beam, I could see that the puncture marks don't match."

"He was bitten by *two different* people?"

The medical examiner shrugged again, the shoulders of his overcoat bunching up around him. "Don't ask me if his blood was drained. Let's not make this a horror movie just yet, okay, gentlemen?"

The officers nodded.

"I'll get him in the lab. Then I can tell you more. But for now, I can definitely say the kid didn't die of natural causes."

Anderson turned back to Winks's mother and Art and Marie. "Again, I'm so sorry. I'm going to need to examine the boy. There is a strange circumstance here that I need to investigate. And I—"

"You mean Rich was *murdered*?" his mother cried.

The ME ran a hand through his gray hair. He lowered his voice to just above a whisper. "It . . . wasn't natural causes. I'm so sorry. I can tell you more later."

Mrs. Winkleman let out a cry and knocked her bourbon glass off the table. It hit the floor and bounced twice but didn't shatter.

Anderson lowered his head, turned, and walked out

of the house. He had a stooped kind of walk, as if what had happened was weighing him down.

The plainclothes cop cleared his throat loudly, to get everyone's attention. "I'm Detective Emanuel Batiste." He pointed to the uniformed cop. "He's Sergeant Anthony. We need to hear more about this visitor Rich received. This girl." He raised his eyes to Art. "Do we need to wake up your son? Did he get a good look at the girl?"

Art appeared horrified at the idea of waking Spencer. He raised a hand as if signaling *halt*. "No," he said. "Spencer didn't see her. We already questioned him. Spencer was in his room. He says he only heard them. He never saw the girl."

I was tempted to tell Batiste that he should talk to Morgan Marks. But I stopped myself. I had no proof that Morgan had been here. It was just a guess on my part.

I was sure the police would get around to questioning everyone Winks knew, including Morgan. It wouldn't be right of me to send them after her with no proof at all.

Besides, the whole *vampire thing* was weird and terrifying. How could I accuse Morgan? She is beautiful and likes to hang out with every guy we know. But so what?

Who wouldn't want that kind of attention from a bunch of guys?

Just because she is a flirt. Or maybe even a total

slut. That didn't make her a . . . I could barely think the word . . . *vampire.*

"Maybe your son can remember what Rich and the girl talked about," Batiste said. "Any clue at all . . ."

"He's only four," Art said. "I'm sure he's scared already. Tonight was traumatic for him. We're going to let him sleep."

"Can you talk to him in the morning?" Marie suggested.

Batiste exchanged a glance with Sergeant Anthony. "Yeah. Sure. Tomorrow will be fine. We don't want to traumatize the little guy. But he seems to be the only witness."

"This isn't happening," Winks's mother said, shaking her head. Her cheeks were puffy and tear-stained. A fresh glass of bourbon trembled in her hand.

Batiste turned to Delia and me. "Do you have anything to add? You came late. You discovered the body. Anything else? Do you know anything else that might explain . . . *anything?*"

"Can you give us a list of his friends?" the other cop asked.

Before we could answer, Delia's phone rang. Her ringtone sounds like an old-fashioned telephone bell. It made us both jump. The phone slipped from Delia's hand

and bounced onto the couch.

She bent to pick it up. It continued its steady ring.

Delia stared at the screen and her eyes went wide. "Omigod!" she cried in a high, shrill voice. "Omigod! It's Winks! Winks is calling!"

26

JULIE CONTINUES

I pictured Winks's still body, sprawled on its side under the hedge down by the curb. *Winks is dead*. My brain froze on those words as I watched Delia swipe the screen, accepting the call, and raise the phone to her ear with a trembling hand.

"H-hello?"

Fumbling to take the call, she had put the phone on speaker, and we all heard the raspy growling voice at the other end:

"Who's next? I'm still hungry!"

Detective Batiste dove forward and grabbed the phone from Delia's hand. He raised it to his ear and shouted, "Who *is* this? Who are you?"

We all heard the caller's cold laugh. Then a click. The call was ended.

"Someone has his phone," Batiste murmured, gazing at the screen. "Someone took Rich's phone."

"Can you hit redial?" Sergeant Anthony suggested.

Batiste punched the screen, then waited. "It went straight to Rich Winkleman's voice mail." He handed the phone back to Delia.

Hearing Winks's voice on the phone message made her start to cry again. I dropped down beside her and tried to comfort her. But it was all I could do to fight back the tears, too.

Chills rolled down my back, and, even though the room was warm, my teeth began to chatter. Shock, I guessed. Shock and horror and disbelief.

And then, Spencer's bedroom door swung open, and the little guy came walking out, rubbing sleep from his eyes. He gazed around the room, saw the crowd of strangers, and made a beeline to his mom.

"Spencer, go back to bed," she said. She took his shoulders and started to turn him around gently.

But he stepped away from her grasp. "Did they find Winks?" he asked in a tiny voice. "Is Cousin Winks okay? Can he come tuck me in?"

Heartbreaking. And now the tears were rolling down

my cheeks, and I couldn't help it. I started to sob.

I didn't hear what Art and Marie said to Spencer. But I saw Art pick him up and carry him to his room.

Detective Batiste stood over Delia and me. "I think you two should go home to your parents," he said softly. "I want to talk to everyone tomorrow. But for now, I think you need to go home and get some rest."

I wiped the hot tears from my eyes with the back of my hand. I stood up and helped Delia to her feet. Some ringlets of her hair had fallen over her face, but she made no effort to push them away.

"Do you two need help getting home?" Sergeant Anthony asked.

I shook my head. "I can drive. Thanks."

I glimpsed Winks's mother, sitting so still at the table, frozen like a statue. Her hand gripped her glass, but she made no effort to drink from it. Just stared at the wall, her face a total blank.

Then Delia and I were out in the night, the ground shiny and wet with dew, the air carrying a chill, the trees black against the purple sky and still as death.

An ambulance stood at the bottom of the driveway. I grabbed Delia's arm as I saw two white-uniformed medics trying to slide Winks's body into a big black plastic bag. A body bag.

A cry of horror escaped Delia's mouth. I gripped her arm tight in case she started to faint or something.

"He's going to sit up," Delia whispered, to herself more than me. "Watch. He's going to sit up and say it was all a joke."

But no. The medics were having trouble. Winks's body slid out from the bag and hit the ground heavily.

Headlights swept over the whole scene, putting the two medics in a spotlight so that their white uniforms gleamed brightly and their troubled faces came into focus.

A car, one of those tiny, square Fiats, stopped sharply and edged to the curb. The driver's door opened, and a girl climbed out. She left the headlights on and the motor running and came running toward the medics.

In the yellow circles of light, I recognized Morgan. She ran hard toward the medics by the hedge, her hair flying behind her. She was nearly there when she spotted Delia and me.

She stopped. "What's going on?" she cried. "Is someone hurt?"

Before I could answer, she turned and saw Winks's face, saw the two uniformed men trying to slide him into the bag again. Saw him. Saw his closed eyes. Saw his legs disappear into the long body bag.

"NOOOOO!" her shriek pierced the deep silence of the night. She pressed her hands to her cheeks and turned away from the sight of the dead body. Turned to Delia and me. "Omigod! It's Winks? It isn't Winks—is it?"

Morgan burst into loud, body-shaking sobs. She dropped down beside the hedge. "No. It can't be. No. No. No. Not Winks."

Delia and I hurried over to her. She raised her face to us, already swollen with tears. "He . . . he was the only one . . . ," she stammered. "He was one of the only ones to be nice to me."

She covered her face and sobbed.

Delia and I exchanged glances. I knew what Delia was thinking.

Either Morgan was an extremely emotional person—or she was putting on quite a show. After all, Morgan had only known Winks for about two weeks.

Had she really felt that close to him so quickly?

Delia had no idea that Winks and Morgan had any kind of relationship at all. We all kept it from her.

We knew Winks wanted to win the bet he had made with Zane and Liam. We knew he had seen Morgan a few times. And we knew Winks had planned to break up with Delia.

But none of us wanted to be responsible for bringing

the bad news to Delia. And here was Morgan, acting heartbroken, as if she had lost the love of her life.

Or was I being unfair?

Her tears were real. And her chest-racking sobs seemed real, too.

I heard footsteps on the gravel driveway and turned to see some others leaving the house. Batiste had Mrs. Winkleman's arm, and she leaned on him as they made their way toward the patrol car at the curb.

Sergeant Anthony followed behind. When he spotted Morgan beside the body bag on the ground, he hurried over to her. "Are you okay?" he asked.

Morgan lowered her hands from her face and nodded.

Sergeant Anthony blinked. Maybe he was surprised by how beautiful she is, even when crying. "Did you know him? Are you a friend?" Anthony demanded.

Morgan nodded. "I was driving home. I saw the ambulance. I . . . I didn't know." She turned to Delia and me, and screamed, "What happened? What happened to him?"

Anthony crouched beside Morgan and placed a hand on the shoulder of her jacket. "We don't really know," he said softly. "Your friend . . . I'm sorry . . . Your friend . . . He was murdered."

Morgan let out a choking gasp and covered her face with both hands again.

"We don't know much more than that," Anthony murmured.

I watched Mrs. Winkleman climb beside Batiste in the front of his patrol car. They drove away.

Something caught my eye at the far side of the house. I turned and peered through the trees that dotted the front lawn.

"Whoa," I murmured as I spotted someone hunched against the wall of the house. Someone standing very still. Watching us.

In the square of orange light from the side window, I caught a good view of him. He was weird-looking. He had white-blond hair, closely cropped and spiked. And in the light, his eyes flashed, and I saw that they were silvery, almost no color at all.

He wore a long, black overcoat and pressed against the house as he watched us with those strange, almost blank eyes.

"Hey—!" My voice came out in a choked whisper. "Hey—" I called to Sergeant Anthony.

He turned away from Morgan, his face showing confusion.

"Over there," I whispered. "Against the house. A man. Who *is* that?" I pointed.

Anthony climbed to his feet and followed my gaze.

No one there.

The guy had vanished into the shadows.

27

DEAR DIARY:

I am refreshed. I feel young and alive again.

And feeling young and alive is almost as good as being young and alive. Ha.

I waited so long, too long, I believe. I did my best to hide my weakness, my tiredness, my grayness, my feeling that every move I made was a struggle.

Maybe some of my new friends saw the change in me, the lack of spirit, my inability to focus, my feeling of being far away, alone in a world of shadows. But I did a good job of hiding my true feelings, as I always do.

If anyone noticed that I had faded a bit, they probably thought I was just depressed. Or had private matters on my mind. No one really wants to go too deep.

Sure, girls enjoy heart-to-heart talks, but no one really wants to go as deep as the heart. No one really wants to know the ugly truth behind your smile.

So I waited until I couldn't bear it any longer, Diary. And now I feel the life flowing through me. I feel whole again. I've regained the energy I need. And the hope and strength. I feel real and normal, as if I really had a heartbeat.

Yes, I am high, high from my meal. But I know that even when I come down, I will be able to smile and talk and be with my new friends and have the energy I need to continue to fool them, to keep my secret.

How do I feel about Winks?

Mainly disappointment. Yes, he was tasty and sweet as nectar. But it didn't go as I had planned.

I am not an impulsive person, Diary. I like to plan, to map out my thoughts and ideas about my future, about how I must act, since I am not like the others.

My plan was to save Winks, save the big teddy bear, with all his fine, sweet-flowing blood . . . save him for one big, delicious moment of celebration.

A party. That's what it was going to be, Diary. A

Winks party just for me and me alone.

How disappointing to drink only half. And in such a gulping hurry.

Yes, it revived me instantly. Yes, it made my mind soar, my whole body tingle with the current of life. But, how disappointing to have to settle for a single meal when I had hoped and planned for a banquet.

Well, I shouldn't complain, should I? The cup was half full. Ha.

Yes, there will be tears now. Winks was well-liked. He was a likable guy. Likable and fun-loving and good-natured . . . and sweet. And now the tears will flow. Mine, too.

I have feelings.

It's just that sometimes my needs outpace them.

But I will cry for Winks, along with his friends, along with his family. I'll be as sad and shocked and horrified by his murder as much as anyone in the room. And I will bury my secret so deep in the dark that no one will guess . . . no one will suspect that Winks died because of me.

Winks was sacrificed for me. And my hunger.

There are other surprises, Diary. Surprises for me, too. I mean, isn't it curious how satisfying my hunger *always makes me more hungry?*

Curious and frustrating.

But, I don't need to tell you; Winks's friends are here for when I need to feed again.

PART FOUR

FIVE YEARS EARLIER

28

NARRATED BY MORGAN FEAR

My main way of communicating with my mother is with a sarcastic eye roll.

She asks a question. I roll my eyes.

She makes a comment. I roll my eyes.

She asks me to do something. You get the idea.

It's a very efficient form of communication, and it even saves some arguing time.

My delightful mother, Amelia Fear, likes a good family discussion—especially if it's a talk in which we criticize what I'm doing and tell me that I am wrong. A long sarcastic eye roll puts an end to most discussions and saves me more than a little grief. And no shouting match between the two of us is very good for my throat and vocal cords.

Of course, Amelia Fear's intention is always to improve me, and I guess I need a lot of improvement, since she seldom lets up. Sadly, her idea of improvement is to make me more like *her* and less like *me*.

Am I being too hard on her? Maybe. I think most sixteen-year-old girls are hard on their parents, and I think they have every right to be. Parents need to know when you are ready to separate from them, when you need time to be on your own, without their watchful eyes and their unnecessary comments and suggestions.

So I was brushing out my hair in front of my dresser mirror, getting ready to go pick up my friend, the other Morgan, Morgan Marks. My mother was stuffing a pile of folded-up laundry into my closet.

"I don't know how you can do that to yourself, Morgan," she said. "You're such a beautiful girl."

I rolled my eyes. I knew what was coming.

"You have the most beautiful red hair, such a gorgeous color. Why cover it up and ruin what is special about you?"

I rolled my eyes. "I like it, Mom."

"I know why you like it," she persisted. "So you and that other Morgan can be twins. But you are special. Why do you want to look like her?"

"We're soul twins," I said. I knew she hated when I

said that, so I tried to say it a lot.

"Soul twins doesn't mean you have to be *identical* twins." She brushed something off the shoulder of my black sweater. "Look at you. Dressed in black. Black hair. Blue lipstick. That awful ring in your nose. Blue fingernails. What are you supposed to be?"

I shrugged. "It's a look." I set down the hairbrush and picked up my car keys.

I could see Mom in the mirror. She was frowning as she stared at my reflection, biting her bottom lip. "Is that what they call Goth?"

"I guess." I turned to leave. "Don't worry, Mom. It's just a phase I'm going through."

It was supposed to be a joke, but she didn't laugh.

"You could go to one of those Comic-Cons," Mom said. "And you wouldn't need to wear a costume."

I laughed. "Good one, Mom." She can be funny when she wants to. She's actually very sharp, especially when she's on my case. What a pain.

I think I must get my dry sense of humor from her. Also, she really can figure out people quickly. Sometimes I think she is a mind reader. She seems to know what people really mean when they say things, and I can do that, too.

And Amelia Fear has a dark side. She tries to hide it

from me. But I see her brooding looks and can read her cold thoughts on her face.

I'm a member of the Fear family. And it took me a long time to accept the fact that Fears aren't like other people.

She followed me out of my room. "Where are you going? To meet your twin?"

I rattled the car keys in my hand. "Yeah. I said I'd pick her up at her job."

"She has a job? Where?"

"Behind a frozen yogurt stand at the mall." I grabbed a black jacket from the front closet.

"It would never occur to *you* to get a job," Mom said. "Something to do after school."

Now she was trying too hard to be obnoxious. "Morgan's family has money problems," I said. "She has to pitch in."

"What does her father do?" Mom asked.

But I was out the front door, slamming it behind me.

It was a cool day for spring. The gusts of wind were biting and carried a chill. I was glad I brought my jacket. The late-afternoon sun was already dipping behind the trees, casting long shadows over the ground.

I tossed my jacket onto the passenger seat and climbed into the Subaru Outback. This was Dad's car originally. But he got carried away and bought himself a Range Rover, and since Mom drives a small BMW, the Subaru became our third car.

Of course, they wouldn't give it to me. Dad said he wouldn't trust me behind the wheel of a skateboard. That's his idea of a joke. Makes no sense at all. Why should I even bother to tell him that skateboards don't have steering wheels?

They don't say the Subaru is my car, but they let me drive it almost whenever I want. So who cares?

I drove to the Division Street Mall and parked in front of the TJ Maxx. There were only a few other cars in the lot at this side. It's the last mall in Shadyside, and Morgan says it's in trouble. A lot of the bigger stores have closed, and the place is nearly empty except for week-ends.

I stepped through the entrance and felt a blast of cold air. The air-conditioning was on even though it was still cool out. Soft, boring music swirled around me. I walked past a shoe store and a jewelry store and a teen clothing boutique. All were empty.

I saw two women with baby strollers checking out the window of a kiddie store. And a worker in a blue uniform was half-heartedly pushing a broom across the floor down the aisle.

The yogurt stand was at the other end, across from Best Buy. As I got close, I waved to Morgan, but she didn't see me. She was talking to another girl behind the cart.

Morgan and I really could be twins. I mean, I admit it, my mom is right in a way. Being a Goth is kind of like wearing a costume. Cosplay, you know. Morgan Marks and I have the same raven-black hair and silver nose rings and blue lipstick with fingernails to match.

Morgan wore a short black skirt over black tights and a deep purple vest over her black top. And lots of strands of clanky beads.

She's a little overweight and she keeps her hair a lot shorter than mine and shaved on one side. She's been having trouble with her contacts and hasn't been wearing them, and I noticed that she squints a lot, trying to see clearly.

"Hey," I said, stepping up to the counter. "What's up?"

"Have you met Shamiqua?" Morgan asked, motioning to the other girl.

Shamiqua smiled. "Hi. You must be the other Morgan."

I nodded. "Yeah. We're Morgan and Morgan. Weird, huh?"

"Shamiqua is my new best friend," Morgan said.

"That's because she showed up for her shift early."

"It was an accident," Shamiqua said. "It won't happen again."

We all laughed. Morgan slid her backpack over her shoulders. We said bye to Shamiqua and started to walk.

"Easy day?" I asked.

Morgan struggled to untangle the orange and black beads over her vest. "No way. The raspberry ran out and I only had vanilla and mango. And no one ever orders mango."

I laughed. "Did you have any customers?"

"Not really."

We passed three guys about our age. I didn't recognize them. They didn't go to our school. They looked kind of tough.

"If no one buys yogurt, think you'll still have a job?" I asked.

She squinted at me. "You mean they might put me out of my misery? I dunno." She sighed. "I hate having to go to an afterschool job every day. It means I have to spend the whole night doing my homework. I can't see friends or anything."

I grinned. "Doesn't matter. I'm your only friend, remember?"

"Well . . . I might have *more* friends if I didn't have

to work every afternoon. And I might get to spend more time with Lonny."

Lonny is her boyfriend. We have a big disagreement about Lonny. I think he's a creep. And I think the only time he pays attention to Morgan is when he doesn't have some other girl around.

Morgan thinks he's Chris Hemsworth. A superhero. You know. The guy who plays Thor. He *does* look like Chris Hemsworth a little if you squint and ignore his stringy hair and pale, yellowy face. I don't think he's ever seen the sun.

Trust me. The only colorful things about Lonny are his tattoos. He and his pals at the shop spend a lot of time practicing their art on each other. Lonny has a full sleeve of Darth Vader, C-3PO, and other *Star Wars* characters.

He graduated from Shadyside High a few years ago, and he went right to work in the tattoo parlor. It's called INK, INC., by the way. Clever, huh?

Lonny is four years older than Morgan, and he pushes her around like she's his little sister. She doesn't seem to notice. Morgan is very smart about everything but Lonny.

I think she knows how I feel about him, although I'm never totally honest about him. I know if I throw shade on him, she'll just get angry and we'll have a whole thing.

We turned the corner. The exit was straight ahead. "Why doesn't Lonny ever pick you up after work?" I asked.

"You know why," she said. "He can't get away from work. He's there till nine every night." She frowned at me. "Some of us *have* to work. We're not rich . . . like some people."

"Hey, my family isn't rich," I said.

"Ha!"

"Morgan, we're not rich," I insisted. "My dad is the black sheep of the Fear family because he became a tax lawyer."

"Don't pretend you don't have money," she said. "My dad hasn't worked in two years, and my mom keeps having breakdowns and taking to her bed. You have three cars and you live in a huge house in North Hills."

"But it's falling apart," I said. "My dad can't afford to keep it up."

Morgan grabbed my arm and we both stopped and burst out laughing.

"We are having a pity-me contest!" I exclaimed. "Who is the poorest?"

"I could keep it going," Morgan said. "My brother needs braces but we can't afford them. Our car is leaking oil and—"

"Shut up!" I cried. I pressed my hand over her mouth. "Just shut up. You win, okay? You're the most pitiful."

We started to walk arm in arm to the doors. The three guys I'd seen before were hanging out near the exit. One of them had a cigarette hidden between his hands. The guy next to him carried a shopping bag from the grocery store.

As Morgan and I started to pass them, they called out. "Hey, what are you supposed to be?" one guy shouted.

The others laughed as if he had made a great joke.

"Are you witches or something?"

"Hey, you know what rhymes with witches?"

Another burst of laughter. Like donkey hee-haws.

"You dudes are a riot," I shouted. "Look how we're laughing."

"I like the fat one. How about you, Flip?"

"The other one is prettier, but I wouldn't touch her."

"You'd never get the chance," I said.

"'Cause you're into girls? Ha-ha."

Morgan tugged me toward the door. "Let's just get out of here."

I watched the guy named Flip reach into his shopping bag. "Got a present for you. Think fast!"

He tossed an egg at me. I ducked away.

Morgan swiped at it. Missed. The egg smacked her

in the forehead. It cracked loudly, and yellow egg yolk oozed down her face.

"HEY!" she screamed. She swung her backpack around and began to fumble inside it for something to wipe off her face.

The three guys hee-hawed and bumped knuckles.

I raised my left hand and pointed at them. I shut my eyes and began to murmur the words I had memorized. *Time for a little Fear family magic*, I thought.

"Let's get out of here. What are you doing?" Morgan demanded.

But I didn't break the spell. I kept my finger pointed at them and my eyes shut as I recited the words from the old book, the words I had worked so hard to memorize.

Morgan squeezed my arm. "Stop it!" she cried. "No. Stop. What are you going to *do* to them?"

29

MORGAN FEAR CONTINUES

I opened my eyes when I heard the three guys begin to shout. I saw the stunned looks on their faces. And I saw them start to scratch as their skin broke out.

"Oh, wow." Flip began scratching his scalp with both hands. The other two were rubbing their reddening cheeks, scratching their arms, pawing at their stomachs.

Morgan's eyes were wide. "What did you do?"

"It's an itching spell," I said. I watched them writhe and scratch and moan and suffer. "See how their skin has erupted? Their whole bodies will itch for hours."

I pushed her to the door. Their angry shouts followed us.

"Witches!"

"We'll find you! This isn't finished!"

"Ow. Make it stop. Can you make it stop?"

"Come back. Make it stop. My skin . . . Ow . . . My skin."

They were still screaming when the door slid shut behind us. A minute later, I was pulling out of the mall, onto Division Street.

Morgan shook her head. She stared at me as if seeing me for the first time. "Sometimes I forget you're a Fear," she said.

"Sometimes I try to forget it," I replied. I smiled. "But other times it comes in handy. Especially when you're dealing with idiots."

It was evening rush hour. Traffic was backed up.

Morgan was still gazing at me. "I don't believe you did that to them. How?"

"There's a library no one uses," I said. "It's like a hidden room near the attic stairs in my house. It's jammed with old books, all dusty and yellow and crumbling. The Fear family library. Handed down from all my *eeeeeevil* ancestors."

We both laughed. I'm not sure that was a joke. But there was something funny about having evil ancestors. And everyone in Shadyside knew about my family. I mean, the Fear family history was actually taught in ninth grade. Can you imagine?

"I've taught myself a lot of magic," I said, slowing for a red light.

Morgan looked thoughtful. "Do your parents know?"

I snickered. "They don't have a clue."

The light changed. We moved through the cross street. "Do you think you could teach me some spells?" Morgan asked, fiddling with the beads at her neck.

I laughed. "You want to be a witch, too?"

"Of course," she said. "Doesn't everyone?"

"Where are we going?" I asked. "Your house?"

"No. I promised Lonny . . ." Her voice trailed off.

"Promised him what?"

"That we'd pick him up. His car is in the shop, and he's getting off early today."

I made a right onto Park Drive. A little kid on a scooter made a fast stop on the sidewalk and almost toppled over. His mother came running up behind him.

"Can we talk about Lonny?" I said.

She fiddled with the beads. "No. I know how you feel about him. You're wrong."

"You don't know how I feel about Lonny," I said. "Because we never really discuss Lonny."

"We don't have to. I know how you feel, Morgan. You think—"

"I think he's using you."

"Okay. There. You said it. Feel better now?" Pink circles formed on her cheeks. I could tell she was getting angry. I'd gone too far.

"Sorry," I said. "But . . . seriously, Morgan. Do you really think he cares about you?"

The pink circles darkened to red. "Yes. For sure. Of course he does." We drove on in silence for a few blocks. "Know what Lonny is going to do for my birthday tomorrow?" Morgan asked. "He said he's going to tattoo my name on his arm."

"He told you that?"

She nodded. "Doesn't that prove he cares?"

I didn't answer. I thought of a few sarcastic things to say, but I held myself back. I didn't say them.

"I can read your thoughts," Morgan said. "Maybe I'm a witch, too. A mind reader. I know you're still thinking bad things about Lonny. But you are so wrong about him."

The tattoo parlor was on the corner at River Road. I made a left turn and was pleased to see a parking space right in front.

I shut off the engine and we climbed out. Morgan brushed back her hair with one hand and straightened her skirt.

The late-afternoon sunlight filled the front window of the tattoo parlor. Above the door, a red-and-blue neon sign announced INK, INC.

An elderly woman leaning on a walker came out of the little grocery store next door. She had a bag of groceries resting on the tray of her walker. She narrowed her eyes at us suspiciously. Then turned and moved off slowly in the other direction.

Morgan and I stepped onto the sidewalk. We made our way to the front window and, shielding our eyes from the sunlight, peered inside.

And Morgan opened her mouth in a shriek of horror.

30

MORGAN FEAR CONTINUES

Morgan raised her fists to pound on the glass. But I grabbed her arms and held her back.

I saw what made her cry out. It was Lonny, tilted back in his tattoo chair with a girl on top of him. She had long blond hair and was wearing short shorts. Her legs sprawled over his and they were, shall we say, being as intimate as two people can be who are wearing clothes.

Yes, they were entwined in each other, Lonny's arms around her waist, holding her down, their mouths locked together in a long kiss.

"I'm going to *kill* him!" Morgan cried.

I held on to her. She struggled to break free, to get to the door. She wanted to barge in, break them up, scream and cry at Lonny.

"No," I said. "No. Morgan—no."

I held on till she stopped struggling. She let out a long sigh and her body slumped, like a tire deflating.

I pulled her back, away from the window. "Not now," I said. "Don't go in there. Don't do it. Not till we have a plan."

I was surprised by the tears that trickled down Morgan's face. I guess I didn't really know how much she cared about Lonny. So I didn't take any pleasure in knowing that I was right about him.

Lonny was seriously a creep.

I told you so. I told you so.

I thought it, but I didn't say it.

I didn't like to see my best friend in the world so upset and miserable. Lonny would have to pay. My devious mind was spinning with ideas.

I dragged Morgan to a Starbucks on the next block. We got lattes and took a table against the back wall. The place was nearly empty at five in the afternoon. Just a young woman wearing earbuds, typing away on a laptop, and two kids and a nanny having big chocolate chip cookies and juice.

Morgan had stopped crying, but her cheeks were still wet from her tears. She tapped her blue fingernails tensely on the tabletop and ignored her latte.

I sat across from her, cradling my cup between my hands. We didn't talk for a long while. I was still thinking hard, scheming, trying to come up with the perfect plan to avenge my friend.

Finally, Morgan broke the silence. "Happy birthday to me," she murmured under her breath. "I could kill that jerk. I feel like a total fool."

"Shut up," I said. "You're not a fool."

"He knew I was coming to pick him up," she said. "He knew I was coming."

"I guess he forgot," I said.

Morgan spun the latte cup in her hand. "I wanted to strangle him. I really did."

"I have a better plan than strangling," I said. I couldn't keep a smile off my face.

She eyed me suspiciously. "What kind of a plan? If it doesn't involve strangling, I probably won't like it."

I took a sip of my drink. I'd poured too much sweetener in. "I want to do something special for your birthday," I said.

"Like strangle Lonny?"

"Shut up about strangling. I want to do it at Lonny's tattoo parlor."

She stared at me, one hand twisting the beads at her neck, waiting to hear the rest.

"Let's give each other a tattoo and make it a surprise," I said.

Her face twisted in confusion. "Excuse me?"

"You surprise me, and I'll surprise you," I said. "We'll give each other a small tattoo, and we won't tell what it is until we do it."

She thought about it. "Tattooing is hard. You can't just pick up a needle and tattoo someone."

"Lonny will show us what to do," I said. "He can do most of it. The main thing is, we'll surprise each other."

Her dark eyes flashed. "I like it. Only one problem. How does that help me get back at Lonny?"

I tapped the back of her hand. "Don't worry," I said. "I have a plan for him."

31

MORGAN FEAR CONTINUES

Lonny was setting up his equipment when Morgan and I walked in after lunch the next afternoon. The shop had just opened, and we were the only ones there.

I saw the look of surprise on his face when he saw us. He quickly replaced it with a smile and stepped forward to give Morgan a quick hug. He nodded to me. "Hey, what's up?"

Before I could answer, he turned back to Morgan. "I thought you were going to come pick me up yesterday."

Morgan clenched her fists at her sides. But she kept the steady, blank expression on her face. "Sorry. I . . . uh . . . got hung up."

"No problem," Lonny said. "I got a ride."

Two pink circles formed on Morgan's cheeks. She

flashed me a quick glance. She wanted me to take charge here. I could see she couldn't control her anger much longer.

"It's Morgan's birthday," I said. "And—"

"Oh, yeah." Lonny suddenly remembered. "Happy birthday, babe."

Babe?

"We want to do something special for her birthday," I said. I motioned to the tattoo chair. "We want to give each other tattoos. And we're going to surprise each other. We're not going to tell what they are."

Lonny rubbed the stubble of a beard on his cheeks. "You mean you want to do it yourselves?"

"Well . . . kinda," I said. "We thought you could help. You know. With the needle and everything."

He thought about it for a few seconds, his eyes on Morgan. "Awesome idea," he said finally. "Totally awesome. Sure, I'll help." He moved to the equipment and lifted a large needle attached to a hose. "I'll even give you the employee discount."

Morgan couldn't hold back. "You're going to *charge* us?"

He shrugged. "I kinda have to. My boss keeps track of the ink and stuff."

Lonny had obviously forgotten about his birthday

promise. That he was going to tattoo Morgan's name on his arm. That had to be a lie from the start.

A funny picture flashed into my mind. I suddenly saw Lonny with the words *I'm with Stupid* tattooed on his forehead in black and red.

He was saying something to Morgan, but I didn't hear it. He turned and raised his shirtsleeve, showing off his *Star Wars* tattoo sleeve. "I designed it," he said, "and Mickey, my boss, did the art. It took two weeks."

Morgan just stared at it.

"Awesome," I said.

"I submitted it to *Inked* magazine," Lonny said, pulling his shirtsleeve back into place. "They'll probably want to do a spread on me."

Yes. For sure. It's all about Lonny.

"Who wants to go first?" he asked.

I dropped into the chair before Morgan could answer. "I want to get the first tattoo," I said. "I can't wait to see what Morgan has in mind for me."

Lonny grinned. "I know what it's going to be. It's going to be a big red heart, and it's going to say *Morgan and Morgan*." He laughed.

"Shut up, Lonny," Morgan snapped. "Don't be dumb. I have a nice idea for Morgan."

"Let me set it up," he said. He set down three little

cups in a row on the table. Then he filled each cup with a different-colored ink. He pulled a couple of bottles from a drawer. I saw that one of them was skin lotion.

"Let's get your skin clean and smooth, Morgan," he said, taking my arm.

"Just the backs of her hands," Morgan told him.

"No problem." He rubbed lotion over the back of my hands with a cotton cloth.

He turned to Morgan, who was watching over his shoulder. "Tattoos bleed while you're doing them. So you use this to wipe the blood away as you work." He squeezed some kind of gel from a tube onto another piece of cloth.

Then he flipped a switch and the equipment started to hum. He raised a needle, flipped another switch, and it made a whirring sound and buzzed in his hand. "Do you know which color you want?"

Morgan eyed the ink cups on the table. "Just blue."

Lonny nodded. "Okay. Remember, keep your hand steady. If you slip—"

Morgan backed away. "You know, maybe you should do it for me, Lonny. I don't want to mess it up."

I knew this would happen. I know Morgan so well and her total lack of confidence. But that's okay. Lonny could go ahead and do my tattoo. It wouldn't change my plan at all.

"Go ahead, Morgan," I said. "Tell me. What's my tattoo?"

She kept her eyes on the needle in Lonny's hand. "Little bluebirds," she said. "I want to tattoo a tiny bluebird on the back of each of your hands."

I couldn't hide my surprise. "Bluebirds? Why?"

"Because you are so free. You are the freest person I know. Your spirit is free as a bird."

I felt a stab of emotion in my throat. "That's . . . very sweet," I said softly.

Lonny placed my left hand on the table, and he spread my fingers out. The needle whirred and spun in his hand. He dipped it in the blue ink.

"It stings," he said. "But you can take it. Just don't move your hand."

"I'll show you what I want," Morgan told him. She unfolded a sheet of paper. She had drawn a bluebird on it with its wings raised.

And that's what I got. Two tiny bluebirds, blue outlined in black, on the backs of my hands.

A little surprise for my parents. But the tattoos were tiny and they were *my* hands, and I didn't care if they both had fits.

Besides, I didn't realize it at the time, but I wouldn't be alive to show it to them.

32

MORGAN FEAR CONTINUES

Two bluebirds. Beautiful. Lonny admired his work and rubbed my hands with alcohol to wipe away any germs, then another layer of gel. My hands throbbed, but he said the pain wouldn't last long.

Morgan's turn.

I had a *delicious* plan for Morgan.

She started to sit down in the chair, but I motioned her away.

Lonny was leaning over a sink against the back wall, cleaning his needle.

"What's my tattoo going to be?" Morgan asked.

I raised a finger to my lips to silence her. Then I turned and pointed at Lonny. I began to mumble the words of the spell I had memorized the night before.

A new spell. Exciting for me, but also very stressful. What if I messed it up?

Morgan opened her mouth to speak, but I motioned again for her to shut up. Her eyes locked on mine as if she were trying to burn inside my brain and see what I was doing.

I mumbled the words quickly, so low that Lonny didn't hear.

And when his knees folded and his eyes closed and he slumped against the wall, I darted forward and caught him under the shoulders before he could fall.

"Help me," I shouted to Morgan. "Grab him. Help me put him in the chair."

Morgan hesitated, then hurried over and grabbed Lonny's other arm. "What are you *doing*?" she cried. "What on earth—?"

"It's a sleep spell," I said. "Hurry. Get him into the chair. On his stomach. I . . . I don't know how long the spell will last."

"This is crazy," Morgan murmured. But she wrapped her hands around him, and we dragged him to the chair.

"Stop," I said. "Let's get his shirt off. Hurry."

"Huh?" Morgan squinted at me. "What exactly—"

"No time," I said. "I really don't know how long he'll be asleep."

It was a struggle, but we pulled his shirt over his head. Then we dumped him onto the chair, tilted the chair all the way back, and rolled Lonny onto his stomach.

His arms hung limply down to the floor. They were totally tattooed and his shoulders were covered in ink. But his back was clean.

I grabbed a needle and fumbled with the switches on the unit until I got it to hum to life.

"What are you doing?" Morgan demanded, hands pressed against her waist. "Tell me!"

"It's your birthday surprise," I said. My voice came out high and shrill because of my excitement. *Am I really going ahead with this?*

"Please," Morgan pleaded. "Explain. Tell me."

"I'm going to make Lonny keep his promise to you," I said. "I'm going to tattoo your name across his back."

Morgan gasped. "Are you *serious*?"

I laughed. "Of course, I'm serious. He promised you, didn't he?"

"But . . . but . . . you can't . . . You—"

"Watch me," I said. I lowered the needle to the black ink cup. Got it whirring. Pressed it to his back. It pierced his skin, and I made a short black line.

I motioned to Morgan. "Help me. Hold him down. This is harder than I thought."

She hesitated. "I don't think I want to help."

"Come on, girl. Don't spoil it!" I cried. "This is your birthday treat!"

Lonny was breathing softly, his mouth open a little, eyes shut. I pressed the needle against the pale skin of his back. "Oops."

The needle slipped. I jerked the needle away from the puncture mark I had made. Bright red blood spurted up from Lonny's back.

Morgan let out a scream.

More blood splashed up. Had I hit an artery or something?

I glimpsed a spot of blood on the back of my hand. Without thinking, I raised the hand to my mouth and licked the blood off.

"Mmmmmm."

A river of bright red blood trickled down the crease in the middle of Lonny's back. I dipped a finger in and tasted some more. "Hey, tastes good," I murmured.

Lonny breathed softly and didn't move.

I brought my head down and licked some warm blood off his back. It felt so good on my tongue, and the sweet-sour iron taste made me crave more.

"Morgan? What are you *doing*?" Morgan shrieked at me. "Have you gone crazy?"

I licked more blood off his back. So tangy. So . . . satisfying.

"Morgan, come try it," I said, waving her over. "I never knew . . . I mean, I never knew it was so *delicious*."

The flow of blood slowed. A long line of it had already dried on Lonny's skin. I took the razor he uses to shave the skin and dug another cut, a long horizontal line just below his shoulders.

A new fountain of blood splashed up. I leaned over, let the warm liquid flow against my lips, and took a long drink.

"You're sick!" Morgan cried. "This is sooo sick! You really are a Fear!"

She grabbed my arm and tried to pull me away. I jerked my arm away from her and licked the warm blood—so tasty and delicious and real—like drinking life itself.

I took the razor and sliced another deep cut. I wanted the tasty nectar to be *fresh*, fresh and hot.

"Stop it! Are you some kind of *vampire*?" Morgan shrieked. "Stop it! Stop it!"

"Try it," I rasped, my voice deep and hoarse, like an animal voice. "Try it, Morgan. Try it."

"Noooooo!" she screamed, backing away, hands pressed to her red cheeks. "No! Morgan—please!"

The blood spurted up. I drank it like at a water fountain. So rich and warm and thick. It gurgled down my throat, splashed over my lips. I knew my face was dripping with the hot blood . . . Lonny's hot blood. But I didn't care.

"I never knew . . . ," I growled at my friend, in a voice I'd never heard before, a creature-voice from deep inside me. "I never knew . . . I never knew."

33

MORGAN FEAR CONTINUES

We squealed away from the curb. I didn't remember if we closed the shop door or not.

I let Morgan drive. I felt too insane to get behind the wheel, the life force pumping through my body, the life force from Lonny's blood. I felt crazy and giddy and dizzy, far beyond being drunk. I wanted to sing and scream and dance and fly.

I felt as if I was floating outside my own skin.

I had washed the blood off my face in the little sink in the back. But the front of my clothes was stained dark. And somehow, I could feel the thick liquid clotting in my hair.

Morgan had her eyes straight ahead on the road. She gripped the steering wheel tightly with both hands, like an old person driving. Her lips were pressed tightly together. She didn't say a word until the tattoo parlor was several blocks behind us.

"Slow down," I said. "You're going eighty."

A hoarse cry escaped her throat. "You killed him, Morgan. You killed Lonny!"

"I couldn't help it," I said. "I just . . . couldn't stop."

"Look at you," she said. "Covered in blood. You killed him. You killed Lonny."

I was floating. So happy. Ecstatic. I'd never felt this way before. I wasn't going to let her bring me down.

"I couldn't help it," I said. "I . . . I couldn't stop. I didn't even think. I just . . . I just had to do it. I was as shocked as you. Really."

"You . . . you were like an animal, devouring your prey."

I thought about it. I tried to feel a little bit guilty. But I couldn't.

"I'm a Fear, Morgan. I'm not like other people."

We drove in silence for a long moment. I could see that Morgan was trembling. Her whole body was quivering . . . in horror.

"You should have tried it," I said. "You're always so scared. You're like paralyzed when it comes to anything new."

"Anything *new*?" she screamed. "You *killed* him! Doesn't that mean *anything* to you? You killed Lonny. You took a human life."

"I know. I know," I said. "But . . . but he was not a good person. And it tastes so good."

"You're a *monster*!" she cried. She kept her eyes straight ahead on the road, as if she was afraid to look at me. "A monster."

"Look out. You almost hit that woman," I warned, grabbing the wheel.

"I—I can't live with this," she stammered. She made a sharp left turn, cutting off an oil truck.

"Watch out!" I screamed. "You'd better let me drive."

"No way," she said. "We've got to get you help, Morgan. I can't live with this. We have to find someone to help you—" She spun the wheel hard.

"What are you going to do?" I cried. "Where are we going?"

"To the police. I don't know where else to go. Maybe they'll know what to do."

"Stop!" I screamed. "Let me out! You can't turn me in to the police! We're sisters, remember?"

"No. No, we're not. We're not sisters. You're a *monster*! You . . . you killed Lonny. I have to do this, Morgan."

"The police? You're joking," I said. She couldn't be

serious—*could* she? She would turn her best friend in to the police? Just because I had an accident with a tattoo needle?

"What do you want me to do?" she said. "What do you expect? Do you expect me just to keep it a secret?"

"Yes," I said. "No one needs to know—"

"But I know!" she screamed. "I'll never stop seeing it. I'll never stop seeing you lapping up Lonny's blood like a dog. Letting it pour over your face and drip from your lips. I-I'll see that for the rest of my life!"

Her words were bringing me back to earth. I felt my energy slipping. My body suddenly seemed heavy. The lights that flashed in my eyes quickly dimmed.

"Morgan, listen to me—" I started.

"No. Just shut up. You need help," she said through gritted teeth. I saw teardrops running down her cheeks. "You need help. The police will get help for you. They'll call your parents. They'll find you doctors. They'll—"

"NO!" I screamed. "I won't go there. NO WAY!"

I grabbed the wheel. I tried to spin it, to turn the car.

She jabbed her elbow into my side. "Let go. Let go. Are you *crazy*? Back away, Morgan."

I shoved her with both hands. "Turn around. Turn around *now*. I'm not going to the police."

She clamped her jaw tight, kept her gaze straight

ahead, and gripped the wheel with both hands.

I shoved her shoulder hard. I clamped both hands around the wheel—and swung it to the right.

She elbowed me again.

I swung the wheel.

I saw her foot slam down hard on the brake.

I heard the squeal of tires before I saw the concrete barrier.

It rose up fast in the windshield. Darkened the glass. And then the sound of the crash boomed like thunder, thunder inside my head, a roar that surrounded me and shut out all light.

The jolt of the collision sent my head shooting back against the seat. Pain throbbed instantly all over my head.

And I felt the car rise up over the barrier . . . felt it lift off the ground. And then I was upside down . . . too terrified, too surprised to scream. Upside down, and I knew the car was spinning over, overturning.

There was darkness. Then there was another hard jolt. Then there was crushing pain.

Before it all stopped. Before it all came to an end, I let out one last painful breath.

And then I lost everything. And knew that I was dead.

34

MORGAN FEAR CONTINUES

Yes, I died hanging upside down in the crushed SUV. I stopped thinking or feeling . . . or breathing. I couldn't move. I had no pulse.

I was dead. And Morgan Marks was dead beside me.

Her mouth hung open. Her eyes stared glassily at the broken windshield, seeing nothing. Her head was slanted, tilted at an impossible angle. I knew her neck was broken.

I was dead, so how did I see her?

The Fears know how to cheat death.

Hanging upside down, I willed my hand to move. The fingers were already numb, and the numbness was spreading. I had little time.

I fumbled for my bag. The strap had tangled around my foot.

My hand gripped the strap and tugged the bag up to me. I gripped it tightly with the other hand. Tore it open. And quickly found the needle, the hypodermic needle I carried but hoped never to use.

When you're a teenager, you don't ever plan to die.

You don't stop to think about it. You don't think you'll ever need the family cure. I carried it at the bottom of my bag and never thought about it—till now.

Yes, the Fears know how to cheat death.

The hypodermic was filled with the precious fluid, the formula my family had perfected over many years, after testing it on corpse after corpse. Yes, it was a formula for reviving life.

I knew it would bring me back. Not exactly as I had been. But it would snap me back. I could breathe. I could move. I could *live*.

I removed the cover and raised the needle to my arm.

I glanced at Morgan Marks, so dead and still, open-mouthed as if protesting what had happened to her. Her hands hung limply down. Her hair pushed against the roof of the car beneath us.

I hesitated, the needle poised at my arm.

I have a whole dose, Morgan. I could share it with you.

I could bring you back, too.

But I don't think I will.

You were my best friend, my twin. But you betrayed me in the end.

You planned to ruin my life. You planned to turn me in.

So I'm going to do what's best for both of us. I'm going to let you rest in peace.

I jabbed the needle deep into my shoulder. I was dead, so I didn't even feel a pinprick. But I could feel the results instantly, feel myself reviving.

My sight returned. The jagged shards of glass in the windshield. Gray light pouring into the car. Morgan suspended upside down beside me. Both of us hanging upside down.

The pain of the crash coursed through my body. I felt the stab of the needle in my shoulder. My hearing snapped back. I heard sirens in the distance.

I tried to speak. "Yes! Yesssss!" My voice a dry croak at first, then back to full volume.

I felt a wave of deep sadness roll over me. *I'm dead. I'm here, but I'm dead. I'll never be the same again.*

The sirens rang louder in my ears.

I pulled the needle from my shoulder and let it fall to the car roof beneath my feet.

I turned to Morgan Marks, poor dead Morgan, and

brushed the hair from in front of her eyes. "I won't forget you," I whispered. "I promise I won't forget you. I'll carry your name with me from now on."

I squeezed her limp, lifeless arm tenderly. Then I unfastened the seat belt that was holding me in place, dropped to my knees on the car roof, climbed out through the broken windshield—and hurried away.

PART FIVE

BACK TO THE PRESENT DAY

35

DELIA NARRATES

Detective Batiste swept a hand over his bald head. He motioned for me to take the chair across the table from him. His pale gray eyes followed me as I set my backpack down and slid into the chair.

I clasped my hands in my lap under the table so he couldn't see that I was trembling. How could I not be tense? Winks was dead. I was up all night. No way I could get to sleep.

A young woman in a blue business suit with a white blouse under the jacket took a chair two seats down from Batiste. She had wavy, brown hair, pale blue eyes, and a nice smile. Her chair squeaked against the floor as she slid it closer to the table.

"This is Lieutenant DeMarco," Batiste said. He stood

up, pulled off his wrinkled gray suit jacket, and draped it over the back of his chair. He sat back down with a sigh.

We were in a small, narrow teachers' meeting room at Linden High, a room I'd never been in before. I knew that Julie had been questioned here earlier, and now it was my turn.

The air was stuffy and warm. There was no window. The room was probably a closet at one time. The long table took up most of the room. I saw a few wooden chairs against the back wall, a half refrigerator that hummed loudly. Someone had tacked a poster on the wall of dogs sitting around a table, playing poker. The only artwork in the room.

I studied the room, I guess, to avoid facing the two police officers.

Batiste cleared his throat. He studied a sheet of paper in his hand. "Delia Foreman. Do we have that right?"

I nodded. "Yes. Do I have to raise my right hand or anything?" I don't know what made me say that. Nervousness, I guess.

Officer DeMarco chuckled. Batiste's face remained solemn. "We just want to talk, Delia. Nothing formal. We set up in here so we could talk to Rich Winkleman's friends. Anyone who knew him at all."

"Maybe someone will be able to help us," DeMarco

said. She slid an iPad out of her bag and placed it in front of her on the table.

"We know this is hard," Batiste said, speaking very softly. His eyes never left my eyes. "Did you get any sleep last night?"

"No. I couldn't," I told him. "I . . . I couldn't stop thinking . . ."

He and DeMarco both nodded. She typed something on her tablet.

"It must be really hard on you," Batiste said. "You two were going together, right?"

Julie must have told them that.

I nodded again.

"How long did you go together?" he asked.

"Since I moved to Linden," I said. In my lap, my hands were wet and ice-cold. "It was like love at first sight, I guess."

"I'm so sorry," DeMarco whispered. She seemed genuine, honest.

"And you were getting along well?" Batiste asked. "No big fights or troubles?"

I squinted at him. Did he think I killed Winks? Did he think we had a fight and I killed him? No way.

"We were in love," I said. "Sure, we had a few arguments. Who doesn't?"

Batiste leaned over the table. His chair groaned under him. "Can you tell us about an argument you and Winks had in the parking lot at Chuckles comedy club?"

I swallowed. *Wow. He did his research fast. How did he find out about that? I know Julie would never have told him that.*

"Some people reported seeing you having a screaming argument," Batiste added.

"Whoa," I said. "It wasn't about anything at all." I pushed my chair back. "Should I get a lawyer? Should I call my parents? Are you really going to accuse me of killing my boyfriend and drinking his blood?"

Batiste waved both hands. "No. Stop. Sorry. Please. Come back to the table. We don't suspect you of anything at all."

"You must be a wreck," DeMarco said. "First, the horror of finding your boyfriend like that. Then being up all night. And then our questions. We really are sorry, Delia."

"But we have to ask the questions," Batiste said. He fiddled with his narrow blue necktie. "We're talking to everyone who knew Rich Winkleman. Just trying to get some clues. We don't really have anything to go on at this point."

"And you might be helpful without even knowing it," DeMarco chimed in.

I scooted my chair back under the table. I brushed back my ringlets of hair. "I'll try to answer, but I don't really know anything. We had a fight in the parking lot that night, but it wasn't about anything. I don't even remember what it was about."

They both studied me.

"It was probably me just being jealous," I added. "I can't help it. I'm the jealous type. Well . . . Winks was my first real boyfriend, see."

I knew I was rambling on, talking too much. I couldn't seem to stop my mouth.

"I have to ask everyone this question," Batiste said. "Where were you the night he was murdered?"

"You mean *before* Julie and I drove to his aunt and uncle's house and found him?"

They both nodded.

"I was at Amber's house. She's another friend. Julie and I were at her house. She can vouch for us."

"We believe you," DeMarco said.

"We'll be talking to Amber later," Batiste said, studying his sheet of paper.

"You three are good friends?" DeMarco asked.

I nodded. "Pretty good. I'm the new girl. Like I said, I only transferred to Linden last September. I think Amber and Julie have been friends since elementary school."

"Transferred from where?" DeMarco asked.

"Walter Academy, in Cincinnati."

She typed something on her tablet. "It's a private school?"

"For girls."

Batiste cleared his throat. I saw drops of sweat on his bald head. It had grown hot in this windowless room, not much air, especially with the door closed.

"So you were at your friend Amber's the whole time? And what did the three of you talk about?"

"I . . . I really don't remember," I stammered. "They'd probably remember better than me. I wasn't paying much attention. I was . . . distracted."

He raised one eyebrow. "Distracted?"

"I kept texting and calling Winks," I said, "and he never answered."

"He was babysitting his cousin," Batiste said. "Was that unusual that he didn't respond to you?" He swatted a fly on the table in front of him. Missed. The fly buzzed up to the low ceiling.

"Totally," I answered. "It wasn't like Winks at all. He always texted me back. Or called if Spencer had gone to bed."

DeMarco typed some more on her iPad. I could see the concentration on Batiste's face. His eyes kept their steady gaze on me, but his mind was sifting through other questions.

He leaned forward again. "One last question, Delia."

I tried to return his stare, but it was far too intense. I lowered my eyes to my lap.

"Did Rich Winkleman have any enemies?"

"Excuse me?" The question took me by surprise. It sounded like something from a murder mystery.

Of course, this *was* a murder mystery.

"Enemies?"

"Can you think of anyone who disliked him? Anyone who maybe even hated him?"

I shook my head.

"Did you ever see anyone get into a fight with Rich? Did you ever see or hear anyone threaten him?" Batiste demanded.

"No one," I said. "Winks was a big, sweet teddy bear. Everyone liked him. He was one of those kids who everyone—"

I stopped. A thought flashed into my mind.

If I hadn't been so nervous, I might have thought of it earlier.

"Oh, wait," I murmured.

Both officers raised their eyes to me expectantly. DeMarco stopped typing on her tablet.

"I just remembered something," I said. "I'm sorry. I guess I just put it out of my mind. It sounded so crazy . . ."

"Just tell us," Batiste said.

"Winks told me about this, I guess, two weeks ago? Someone beat him up. At his job. Some guy was waiting for him at the car wash and beat him up. And Winks lost his job."

Silence. They both stared at me. No reactions on their faces. Then Batiste said, "Someone beat him up? Didn't you think that was important enough to tell us?"

I could feel my face turning hot. I clamped my hands tighter in my lap. I hadn't moved them since I'd sat down. "I . . . I'm sorry," I stammered. "This has all been so . . . horrifying. Like a nightmare. I'm not thinking clearly. My brain is, like . . . exploding."

Batiste scribbled a note on his sheet of paper. "Did Rich describe the guy who beat him up? Did he recognize the guy? Did he tell you anything about him?"

I thought for a long moment. "The guy said he was my stepbrother. That's what Winks told me. But that's crazy. I don't have a stepbrother."

"And you don't know why he would say that?"

I shook my head. "No. It's crazy. It's just . . . crazy."

DeMarco crunched up her face. "You don't have a stepbrother? Is there anyone else in your family who would want to beat Winks up?"

"Of *course* not," I snapped. "No way. I told you, this guy must be crazy or something. I don't know who he is or why he said what he said."

Batiste opened his mouth to ask another question, then stopped. "We're going to have to look into this. I'll send someone to the car wash."

He sighed. "I guess that's enough for now."

"Thank you, Delia," DeMarco said. She tucked her tablet into her bag.

"Sorry I couldn't be more helpful about the guy," I murmured. "I just—"

"That's okay," Batiste said. "We'll check out the car wash. You just gave us our first real clue."

36

DELIA CONTINUES

I stepped into the lunch line at school. I wasn't very hungry. Of course, I'm *never* very hungry. I didn't want to eat, but I had a gnawing feeling, a heaviness, a feeling of emptiness that wouldn't go away.

Winks was gone, and I knew I had to find a way to go on and be as normal as I could be. But I also knew this empty feeling would never leave me. Several times a day, I had to force myself to hold back the tears, and the constant tension, the worry that I'd break down made me tense and tired and edgy.

I wanted to burst out of my own body and just fly free. Escape from myself. I never liked myself that much anyway. My shrimpy body. My babyish, bobbing ringlets of curly hair. My tiny mouse voice. The way I *needed* people . . .

I always wanted to be someone else.

I longed to be confident and pretty with all-American good looks like Julie. Or as driven and talented as Amber. Or . . . as stunningly beautiful as Morgan. But who could even dream of that?

I saw Amber, Zane, and Liam at a table near the front of the lunchroom. I took a deep breath. I knew I had to sit with them. But could I keep myself in control?

All three of them were talking at once. I wondered if they were talking about Winks. Or had they put the awful murder out of their minds? Were they ready to move on? To pretend it didn't happen to one of their best friends?

I suddenly realized someone was calling my name. I looked up and uttered a sharp cry of surprise. I stared across the counter at Liam's mother.

It took me a few seconds to remember that Mrs. Franklin worked as a server in the lunchroom. "Delia, hi." She wore a long white apron over her dark top and jeans. Her light brown hair, mixed with streaks of gray, poked out from under her mesh cap.

Liam never talked about his mother working in the school. I'm not sure why, but I think he was embarrassed about it.

"Mrs. Franklin—" I started.

She narrowed her eyes at me. "How are you doing, dear? Liam told me the whole story. So frightening."

I nodded. "Yes."

"Liam has been in a daze," she said, leaning over the food table. "I don't think he really believes what happened. I don't think any of us do."

"It . . . it's horrible," I managed to choke out.

The other two servers were watching her. Mrs. Franklin suddenly realized she was keeping the line from moving. She shook her head sadly. "Well, pile up your tray, Delia. It's free for you today. I'm sure Winks's death hit you harder than most everyone. Chin up, dear."

I thanked her and put a few dishes on my tray without even looking at them. I knew I wasn't going to eat. I carried the tray to my friends' table and sat down next to Amber, across from Liam and Zane.

They greeted me with grim faces. I could see they were studying me, trying to see how I was doing, how I was handling the whole thing.

"Afraid we can't stop talking about Winks," Amber said, pushing her glasses up on her nose. Her hair appeared stringier than usual. She obviously hadn't shampooed it for a while.

"It's hard to think about anything else," I said quietly. I pushed a fork through the macaroni on my plate.

"This morning in government class, I didn't hear a word Maloney said."

"I *never* do," Zane joked.

Liam jammed the last half of a hot dog into his mouth. He chewed noisily. Then he poked Zane in the side. "Aren't you supposed to do another comedy thing at Chuckles this week?"

"I canceled it," Zane said. He finished a small carton of apple juice. "Who can be funny now?"

"You *never* could!" Liam cracked.

Zane lifted the juice carton over Liam's head and turned it upside down. But it was empty.

Amber turned to me. "Did those two cops question you yet?"

I nodded. "Yes. Friday."

"I talked to them this morning," Amber said. "But I couldn't be helpful at all. I mean, I don't know anything. I don't have a clue. But they kept asking these questions. Like, did they expect me to tell them who the killer was?"

"I didn't have anything to say, either," Liam said, reaching for another hot dog on his plate. "Winks was my best buddy. I told them about our Ultimate Frisbee games and everything. They wanted to know if Winks had an enemy on our team. How stupid is that?"

"The cops didn't seem stupid," I said. "Just clueless."

Amber put a hand on my shoulder. "Were they at least nice to you?" she asked. "Since you and Winks were so close—"

I let out a sigh. "I was in such a daze. I think I was still in total shock. I didn't notice if they were nice or not."

Liam pointed to my tray. "You're not eating your lunch?"

"I'm not very hungry," I said.

"Can I have your pretzel?"

Zane gave him a shove. They both grabbed for the pretzel at once. It broke in two, and they each got half.

Amber tangled and untangled a string of her hair. She was always a very tense person, but now she seemed strung as tightly as a wire. "Here's what I don't understand," she said, lowering her voice to just above a whisper.

I leaned closer to hear. Liam stopped chewing the pretzel.

"Why was Morgan so hysterical over Winks?" she said. "I mean, I heard she just went crazy, screaming and crying. And how long did she know him? A couple of weeks?"

"You're right. She barely knew him," Zane agreed.

"I think Morgan is just very emotional," Liam said. "She's a very emotional person."

"How do *you* know?" Amber snapped.

He shrugged. "I don't." Then a devilish smile spread over his face. "But I'd *like* to."

Amber tossed up her hands. "Even now? Your friend is dead. Can you maybe let it go for just a second?"

I took a breath. "Do you think that Morgan and Winks had a thing? Do you think that's why Morgan went so crazy when he was killed?"

"Of course not," Amber answered quickly. She wrapped her fingers around my wrist. "Winks was crazy about you, Delia. He and Morgan never went out or anything. Winks wouldn't do that."

I studied her. Was she telling the truth? Or was she just trying to make me feel better?

I didn't have long to think about it. Shouting voices at the lunch line made me turn to see what the commotion was. The room suddenly grew quiet.

I saw Morgan bang her tray with a fist. She was shouting at someone behind the counter. Mrs. Franklin, Liam's mom.

Mrs. Franklin leaned over the counter and shouted back at Morgan. Her face was red. She tore off her mesh cap and slammed it against the counter.

Liam and I exchanged glances. *What on earth?*

Liam started to get up. I guess, to go help his mother.

But Morgan swung around and, carrying her tray in front of her, strode angrily toward us. She dropped her tray to the table, pulled out a chair next to Zane, and plopped down.

Her green eyes flashed angrily. She blew a strand of red hair from in front of her mouth. "Well . . . *that* was pleasant," she said.

"What happened?" I asked.

"That woman happened," Morgan muttered.

"Did you know she's my mom?" Liam asked.

Morgan crinkled her face at him. "Don't be funny."

"No. Really," he protested. "She's my mom. What did she say to you?"

Morgan stared hard at him, trying to decide if he was joking. "Well . . . your *mom* said I had too much junk food on my tray. And she told me to put some of it back."

Liam snickered. "That sounds like my mom."

"And what did *you* say?" I asked.

"I said, if you don't want people to eat so much junk food, why do you put it on the counter?"

"She probably didn't like that," Liam said, grinning.

Morgan rolled her eyes. "Then we both started screaming at each other. It got crazy."

"We heard," Amber said.

"I think I told her where she could put her junk food,"

Morgan said. She let out a cry. "It was stupid. I . . . I'm just not myself." She lowered her head. Her hair fell over her face.

"Mrs. Franklin is actually very nice," I said.

"She made one mistake in her life," Zane said. "She had Liam."

We all laughed. It broke the tension. Morgan raised her head and laughed, too.

She tore open a bag of potato chips and raised a handful to her mouth. "Delia, are you okay?" she asked. "How are you doing?"

I shrugged. "Hard to say. I . . . keep wanting to cry. Sometimes I just want to scream."

"It's like a nightmare," Morgan said. "I keep trying to wake up and come out of it. Those cops questioned me for an hour yesterday afternoon."

"What did you say?" Amber asked.

Morgan swallowed the last chip and crinkled up the bag. "What could I say?" she replied. "I told them the truth. I killed Winks and drank his blood."

37

JULIE NARRATES

I really wanted to have lunch with my friends. But Mom needed me to do some paperwork and filing in the principal's office. So I grabbed a tuna fish sandwich and a bottle of ice tea and ate while I worked.

I felt jumpy and out of sorts, like I wasn't really myself. I tried to force all the sad thoughts from my mind, but I just couldn't. The words from the TV news story this morning kept repeating in my mind. No way I could block them or erase them from my memory.

Someone had leaked that the Linden press was calling what happened *the Vampire Murder*. The news story said that Winks's body had been examined and it was totally drained. No blood.

A police officer denied the whole thing. But there was

the story, and someone—whoever examined Winks's body—swore it was true.

Now, how do you stop thinking about *that*?

Especially when it was one of your best friends who was murdered.

The town of Linden is peaceful and small. And when something truly horrifying occurs, I think people are more shocked, more shaken—because it's just not supposed to happen here.

A "vampire" murder? Not in Linden. *No way* that could happen in our little town.

As you can tell, I was awake all last night, thinking about all this. And now, I was still in such an unhappy haze, I realized I'd been putting the files I was collecting in the wrong cabinet.

I was still moving them to the right drawers when I looked up and saw Morgan Marks walk into the office. She wore an emerald sweater that matched her green eyes, over tight-legged black denims. The bright office lights made her creamy skin glow.

Normally, I wouldn't think things like that. But she really was, like, perfect. And she gave me a smile, a warm smile, maybe the first one since I met her that night in the comedy club.

"Hey. Hi," I said, setting a stack of files down on the

front counter. "How are you doing?"

She shrugged. "Trying to keep it real."

I nodded. "For sure." Then there was an awkward pause.

"We missed you at lunch," Morgan said. She snickered. "I freaked out your friends."

I leaned on the high counter. "What do you mean?"

"I told them I confessed to the police that I killed Winks and drank his blood. It was a joke, but you should have seen the looks on their faces. Like maybe they believed me."

I felt a chill at the back of my neck. "It wasn't a very good joke," I said.

She nodded. "Everyone always tells me I have a twisted sense of humor."

"Yeah. Well. That was pretty sick," I said. "Maybe this isn't a good time for jokes."

"I think I was just trying to cover up how scared and upset I am about Winks. You know. Like when people laugh or say stupid things at funerals?"

I stared at her. "I guess." I heard Mom on the phone in the inner office behind me. She was apologizing to some parent about something.

I glanced at the clock. Almost time to go to class, and I hadn't finished my tuna fish sandwich.

"After my stupid joke, Amber mentioned that you are looking for volunteers," Morgan said, sweeping back her hair off her shoulders.

"Volunteers?" I had to think hard. "Oh. You mean for the alumni carnival?"

Morgan nodded. "Yeah. But I have one question. What's the alumni carnival?"

I laughed. "Didn't Amber tell you? It's a big party. They hold it here in the high school, and they invite more than a hundred Linden graduates to come."

She shifted her backpack on her back. "It's like a party?"

"You know, they have a DJ and there's dancing. And there's food, and an auction to raise money for the high school. And sometimes people perform."

"Can I help?" Morgan asked. "I love being on committees and things."

I tried to hide my surprise. Morgan didn't seem like the committee type. But here she was volunteering. Maybe I had her all wrong. Maybe since she is so beautiful and seemed like such a flirt, I misjudged her.

"Sure," I said. "That's awesome. I'll put your name down on the list."

Morgan smiled, but her gaze was on someone behind me. I turned and saw my mom walking over to us from her office. "Morgan, just the person I wanted to see," Mom said cheerily.

Morgan slid her backpack to the floor. "Seriously, Mrs. Hart?"

Mom nodded. "We're having a little trouble gathering your school records. It turns out there were *three* Morgans in your class at Shadyside High."

"Yeah, I know," Morgan replied. "Two girl Morgans and one boy."

"I think it's caused some confusion," Mom told her. "And I think it's why we haven't received your records."

Morgan nodded. She didn't reply.

"The school asked if we could send them a photo of you to help straighten it all out," Mom said.

Morgan thought about it for a moment. "No problem," she said. "Shall we take it right here?"

"Sure. Just stand against the wall," Mom said. She turned and started back to her office. "I'll get my phone."

Morgan backed up to the wall. "This is weird," she muttered to me. She straightened her hair with one hand and adjusted her sweater.

Mom returned with her iPhone. "You take it, Julie. You know I'm a klutz when it comes to this phone." She shoved it into my hand.

I gazed at it. "Mom, you're three phones behind. You need to upgrade."

"I need to *down*grade," Mom said. "These phones are just too complicated."

I turned to Morgan. She was still fiddling with her hair. "It doesn't have to be perfect," I said. "They just want to identify you."

She laughed. "So now you think I'm vain?"

I didn't answer. I leaned my elbows on the counter, raised the phone, and centered Morgan on the screen.

"Smile," Mom said.

I laughed. "Why should she smile? This isn't going in the yearbook, Mom."

I clicked the screen.

"I should turn sideways," Morgan said. "You know, like in a police mug shot."

"Why? Have you done something wrong?" Mom asked. I think she meant it as a joke, but it didn't come out funny.

"I'll take one more," I said. I clicked another one. Then I handed the phone back to my mother.

"I'll send it to Shadyside right away," Mom said. "And we'll straighten out this whole thing with your missing records."

The buzzer blared right above our heads. "We're late," I said. I spun around, trying to remember where I left my backpack.

"Catch you later," Morgan said. "And thanks for letting me be on the alumni party committee."

"It'll be fun," I said. But she had already disappeared into the hall.

I found my backpack where I'd tossed it against the back wall. I hoisted it up and started out of the office.

"Hey, Julie," Mom called from her desk. "Come here a minute. There's something wrong."

"Something wrong?" I turned and strode back to her office. "You mean with your phone?"

She nodded. "Look. Look at Morgan's photos."

I took the phone from her and glanced at the first photo. "Hmmm . . ." I slid my finger over the screen, flipping to the next photo.

"Totally weird," I said.

The office wall was clear and sharp. But Morgan was a complete blur of green and brown. I couldn't see her face at all.

38

NARRATED BY MRS. FRANKLIN,
LIAM'S MOTHER

Wednesday is my favorite day of the week because we serve the mini pizzas. They are easy to prepare. We just put tomato sauce and cheese on top of English muffin halves and bake them at a high heat in the oven.

The kids grab them up like crazy. There are usually only a few left after the lunch period. So they are easy to clean up and not a big deal to take care of.

Thursday is a different story because of the hamburger sliders. They are just as popular. But after lunch hour, I have to spend a long time scraping the grill and cleaning it and making sure it's spotless.

The grease goes everywhere. I have to totally clean the tile backsplash, too, as well as the grill hood.

Eleanor Hadley, my boss, is a perfectionist, and I'm

not. I admit it. So I've been reprimanded more than once for my incomplete cleanup job.

I need this job. Jim has been out of work for longer than I care to think about. So I have to deal with his depression, along with bringing some money into the house. His unemployment is going to run out soon. Then my job will be our only income.

I finished wiping down the grill hood and took a step back to make sure I hadn't missed a grease spot anywhere. That's when I heard footsteps. Someone entering the kitchen.

I jumped, startled, because I thought I was alone. It was nearly five o'clock and I knew the school should be empty by now.

I turned and saw that girl with the red hair and the pretty face. No, beautiful. She had a beautiful face, partly because of those amazing green eyes.

I instantly remembered the screaming fight we'd had at the food counter. Her immediate anger as she lashed out at me, screaming so loud all conversation in the huge room stopped, and everyone turned to stare at us.

Watching her walk past the metal freezers, the refrigerator, the preparation tables, my first thought was that she had come to apologize. I put a smile on my face and turned to greet her. I wished I knew her name. I think she was a new student. I know I'd remember that face of hers.

"You're in school very late," I said.

She stopped a few feet from me. "Too late for you," she said.

I didn't understand what she said. She had her hands down stiffly at her sides and stood very erect, as if she was tense.

"Sorry about our disagreement at lunch the other day," I said. I thought I'd make the first attempt to apologize, perhaps I had gone too far by telling her what she should and shouldn't eat.

Her enormous green eyes gazed at me like headlights. I had this strange feeling of being captured in them.

I waited for her to apologize as I had. But she didn't say a word, just stood there stiffly, giving me the evil eye.

"You really shouldn't be here this late," I said finally, keeping my voice low and calm. "Is there something I can help you with?"

"Yes. You'll help me a lot," she said.

I didn't understand that, either. It was like she was talking riddles.

"I'm very hungry," she said.

I blinked. "Well, you'll have to go to a store or a restaurant or something. There's nothing here. We don't prepare food till morning."

She took a step toward me. I felt a chill of fear at the back of my neck. Did she come here to fight?

"You have a lot of food," she said.

"Now, wait—" I cried, suddenly angry. "You can't come in here this late and ask for food. That's crazy. I'm ready to go home." I narrowed my eyes at her. "What do you think you're doing?"

"You shouldn't have yelled at me," she said coldly, no emotion at all. "You shouldn't have made a fool of me in front of all the others."

"I didn't mean to," I said, backing away from her, from those cold, angry eyes. "I'm sorry. I already said I'm sorry. But—"

"Now I need to feed," she said.

She leaped forward. She was on me before I could take another step back.

"Hey—let go! Get off!" I screamed. My cry rang off the walls of the empty room. I knew no one was around to hear me.

And then I screamed in pain as I felt a sharp stab at my throat. An animal howl escaped my mouth. I knew at once that she had bitten into my neck.

I went down on the floor. She pushed me onto my back. And now her teeth were tearing at my throat, slashing my skin. I felt the warm blood flowing down my neck.

I squirmed and twisted, struggling to get out from under her. But she was so strong . . . so inhumanly strong.

She made gurgling noises as she hungrily dug her teeth deeper and drank, drank my flowing blood. She pressed me to the floor and slurped and drank until she was choking on blood. And then . . .

Then . . .

I don't know what happened then.

I saw the bright ceiling lights high above me. Then they seemed to go out. And the blackness covered me. And I was gone.

39

NARRATED BY LIAM

I brought Zane home with me, planning to work on the drone in my garage. I thought maybe if I kept busy, you know, worked with my hands, did something physical, it would help me stop thinking about Winks for a little while.

But Zane is so hopeless when it comes to building anything mechanical, and the truth was, I really couldn't work up the energy to do anything on the drone. Ever since Winks was killed, I've felt as if I have a heavy weight pushing me down, holding me down, keeping me from moving. From thinking or wanting to do anything at all.

I know I have to snap out of it and try to get back to normal. Mainly because I have no choice—I have to keep living. There's nowhere to hide.

Pretty deep for me, huh?

Well, I've been thinking a lot. Mainly late at night when I can't get to sleep, and I keep thinking about Winks and how he died, how someone or some*thing* punctured his neck and drank his blood.

Where *can* you hide when you're living in a horror movie?

Anyway, we didn't work on the drone. Zane and I ended up tossing a Frisbee back and forth in my backyard and tried to talk about everything else, everything but Winks.

"My dad has a job interview today," I said. My throw went wide, and Zane had to chase it to the back fence.

"Where?" he called. He heaved a line drive at my chest, which I caught easily.

"The travel agency on Lafayette," I said.

"But isn't your dad some kind of engineer? Didn't he work at the Ford plant?"

"The Ford plant moved to Mexico, remember? I think my dad just wants a job. You know. Anything that he can do."

"I guess you won't be having any more Ultimate Frisbee games," Zane said, his voice suddenly so low I could barely hear him.

"You mean without Winks?"

No matter what we talked about, it always came back to Winks.

Zane jumped to catch a throw above his head. "Yeah."

I shrugged. "I guess. I was thinking about trying out for the baseball team."

Zane squinted at me. "Do we have a baseball team?"

I laughed. "It's a well-kept secret. But yes, we have a baseball team. They aren't any good, but at least no one ever goes to their games. So the embarrassment potential is very low."

Zane laughed. The Frisbee toss was loosening us up. He's not any kind of jock. In fact, he hates playing sports because he sucks at all sports. But he was enjoying the exercise, I think. Working off some tensions.

Then Delia showed up.

She wore a white V-neck tee over white tennis shorts. Her face was nearly as pale as her clothes. She walked across my backyard with her shoulders stooped. Her expression was sad, and her cheeks were red, as if she'd been crying.

Poor Delia. I realized that Winks wasn't just a crush. She really was in love with him. And now he was gone, and she was walking slowly toward us like an old lady, her ringlets bobbing lifelessly at the sides of her head.

"Hey, what's up?" I called.

She shrugged. "I don't know if I'm bored or going crazy. Or maybe somewhere in between."

Zane came running over, the Frisbee in his hand. "We all feel totally weird," he said.

"I keep hearing noises," Delia said. "I turn around thinking it will be Winks." She sighed. "How crazy is that?"

"Crazy," I said. "I guess . . . I guess it will take time for all of us." I didn't know *what* to say.

Delia took the Frisbee from Zane and turned it in her hand. "Did anyone hear anything from the police? Did you see any news?"

Zane and I shook our heads. "I haven't seen anything." I glanced at my phone. It was nearly five thirty. Mom's car wasn't in the drive. She was usually home before me.

"Delia, maybe you should come to my stand-up comedy thing next Friday," Zane said.

Delia blinked in surprise. "You're going ahead with it?"

Zane nodded. "Yeah. I changed my mind. I decided I can't just sit around being depressed." He lowered his gaze to the lawn. "Winks loved to laugh. I'm going to dedicate my act to him next Friday night." He raised his eyes to her. "Want to come?"

Delia twisted her face up, thinking hard. "Maybe."

I knew that meant no. She wasn't ready to laugh at anything. And Zane's act is so bad, it makes you want to cry! (Kidding.)

I glanced at my phone. Nearly a quarter to six. Where was Mom? She always came straight home after the kitchen at school was cleaned up.

I texted her. Waited for a reply. Nothing.

"Julie and Amber have been really terrific," Delia said, spinning the Frisbee slowly in her hand. "So understanding."

"That's great," I murmured, eyes on my phone.

"Even Morgan invited me over," she said. "She said I could call her anytime I wanted to talk."

I exchanged a glance with Zane. *Why doesn't Morgan invite ME over?*

My phone buzzed. I glanced at the screen. Mom? No. A guy who sometimes played on our Ultimate Frisbee team. I didn't take the call.

"Listen, guys," I said, pocketing the phone. "I'm a little worried about my mom. She should be home by now."

"Maybe she took your dad to his job interview," Zane said.

"No. She wouldn't do that. Or else, she'd leave me a note or something." I started to the house to get the car keys. "I'm going to drive over to school and see if she's still there. You guys want to come?"

Delia handed me the Frisbee. "I don't think so. I've got to get home. I'm way behind . . . with *everything*. Catch you later." She gave us a little wave, turned, and started down the driveway.

"I'll go with you, Liam," Zane said, following me to the house. "I'm not in a big hurry to get home. My mom is serving some kind of fish for dinner, and I hate fish."

"Why would anyone eat fish?" I said.

So we drove to the high school. We have a hip-hop Pandora station in the car, and I cranked it up high, partly so we wouldn't have to talk about Delia and Winks. And partly because I didn't want Zane to see how tense I was about Mom not showing up or answering my texts.

I knew I was being crazy. She had every right to go shopping or visit someone or stay late at the school. I guess I was super tense because of what happened to Winks, and I couldn't stop thinking that the killer was still out there. Who wouldn't freak out after such a horrifying thing?

I parked in the student parking lot. No other cars in sight. Zane and I climbed out, and I jogged to the teachers' lot on the other side of a tall chain-link fence.

"Isn't that your mom's car?" Zane asked, pointing.

The dark blue Jetta was parked against the fence. "Yeah. She's still here," I said. "Weird."

Seeing the car should have calmed me down a bit, but it didn't.

Zane and I went in the side door, followed the dimly lit hall, our shoes ringing loudly in the emptiness. Down the stairs to the lunchroom.

"No one here. Not even the janitors," Zane murmured.

We were outside the double doors to the lunchroom. I pushed a door open and shouted. "Hey, Mom! Mom? It's me!"

My voice echoed in the huge room. The chairs were all upside down on the tables. The janitors must have washed the floor.

"Hey, Mom—?"

Behind the long line of empty food tables, the light was on in the kitchen.

Zane followed me as I edged behind the food tables

and stepped up to the open kitchen doors. "Hey, Mom—are you here?"

I stepped into the kitchen and nearly tripped over the body on the floor.

"No. Oh no," I moaned. "Noooooooooooo."

40

LIAM CONTINUES

I staggered back. I started to choke. Couldn't breathe.

Mom was lying on her back, arms at her sides, legs outstretched. Her hair had fallen over her face, covered it like a blanket.

But all I could stare at was the gaping red hole in her neck. The skin had been torn open. Blue veins hung out from the deep hole in her throat.

But there was no blood. I saw a tiny brown puddle of dried blood under her head. But her throat . . . her ripped-open throat . . . the gaping pink wound . . . It had no blood.

I heard a sound behind me. Swung around and saw Zane on his knees, vomiting on the floor. Loud eruptions of his horror, his head bobbing up and down.

I had an urge to drop beside my mother, to hug her, to hold her. But that vanished quickly. I couldn't take my eyes off her torn skin, her open throat. It all glowed so brightly under the kitchen lights, as if it wasn't real.

"Mom . . ." I struggled to breathe. My chest felt as if a tight net had closed around it. A wave of dizziness made me grab the wall. "Mom . . ."

And then I glimpsed something move beyond the twin stoves at the far end of the kitchen. A man!

"Hey—" I choked out. I stumbled around my mom and took a step toward him.

He was weird-looking. He had spiky white-blond hair. His face had no color at all. He wore a black shirt and black pants, which made him look even paler.

"Hey—stop!" I uttered.

He raised a hand, as if to wave me away. He narrowed almost-colorless eyes at me.

My chest began to heave. I could feel the anger burning through me. I clenched my fists and moved toward him.

"Stay back, kid." His voice was deep and raspy. "Stay back. I'm warning you." He tensed his body, preparing for a fight.

He killed my mother. Now he's warning me?

The rage burst up from deep inside me, a feeling I'd

never had before. I opened my mouth in an animal roar.

I lowered my shoulder like a football running back and charged across the kitchen. A large metal skillet rested on a wooden table. I swiped it up and raised it as I ran.

The man's weird gray eyes opened wide in surprise as I dove at him. He was pinned against the wall.

"Stay back!" This time his scream sounded desperate.

With another angry animal cry, I raised the skillet high. "You killed my mother!" My voice came out in a shrill screech.

I swung it at his head. Connected. It made a loud *thud* as it smashed into his face. The man's eyes rolled up and he let out a low grunt.

I swung the skillet again and caught the back of his head as he went down. He crumpled in a heap, legs crossed beneath him, then toppled onto his stomach, arms splayed, eyes shut. He didn't move.

My chest felt about to burst. I tried to take a deep breath, but everything felt closed up. I made horrible wheezing sounds, struggling to catch my breath.

The pan fell from my hand and clattered loudly to the floor. The man didn't move. I could see him breathing. But he was out cold.

Was that really me? Did I really do this?

Crazy thoughts.

I spun around. Zane was still on his knees, wiping off his face with the front of his T-shirt.

"I got him!" I cried. "I got the killer."

Zane raised his phone. "Already dialed 911," he said. "They're sending the cops. They're on their way."

My legs felt weak. I grabbed the wooden tabletop to hold myself up.

"Why?" I cried to Zane. "Why? Why did he kill my mom?"

41

LIAM CONTINUES

Time passed in a haze. Zane and I sat at a table in the lunchroom and watched the cops hurry into the kitchen. Then a bunch of medics arrived in their green lab coats, carrying oxygen equipment, I think.

Too late for that. Mom doesn't need oxygen.

It was all a blur to me. A blur of deep sadness and horror, and I was trapped inside it. I didn't see when she came in, but I realized Mrs. Hart, Julie's mom, the principal, had a hand on my shoulder. She was speaking softly, her face close to my ear, so close I could smell her lemony perfume, but I couldn't make out many of her words.

"Your dad is on his way," she said. "Of all things, he had a flat tire."

I nodded. I didn't know what to say to her. I couldn't focus my eyes or my brain.

Zane sat across from me, tapping his fingers on the tabletop. He was nodding his head to some kind of rhythm in his brain. A blue-uniformed janitor had been summoned to clean up Zane's vomit on the floor.

I could hear voices in the kitchen. People all seemed to be talking at once.

"Maybe you want to go to another room to wait for your dad?" Mrs. Hart said softly.

I shook my head. "No. This is okay."

But it wasn't okay.

And when the medics came carrying a large dark gray body bag from the kitchen—my mother—a loud sob burst from my throat and shook my whole body.

No tears. No tears yet. Just that racking sob, followed by a chill down my back. And I wished my dad would arrive.

Zane continued bobbing his head and tapping the tabletop, off in his own world. His eyes were shut tight. I don't know what he was seeing.

I wanted to tell him he could go home. He didn't have to wait.

I didn't know what there was to wait for.

And then, some cops appeared from the kitchen with

the blond-haired killer between them. He was awake. But not walking well and blinking his eyes as if trying to clear them.

They lowered him to a chair at the table beside mine. Mrs. Hart still had a hand on my shoulder, and I felt it tighten when the cops sat the killer down.

The guy shook his head. He was obviously groggy. And in pain. A large purple bump had swelled on his forehead. And the medics had put some kind of pack under his nose to stop it from bleeding.

I recognized Detective Batiste as he stepped out of the kitchen, shaking his head. He glanced around the room, then stepped up to the killer and peered down at him. "Can you talk?" he asked.

The killer nodded. "I can talk." He rubbed the bump on his forehead, groaned, and pulled his hand away.

"Can you tell us your name?" Batiste demanded, leaning over him. "What were you doing here?"

"My ID," the man said in a whisper. "In my back pocket. I'll show it to you." He reached a hand back to the pocket and cried out. "The pain. My head. It's about to explode. Can I have something for the pain?"

Batiste nodded to one of the medics against the wall. "You can have something after you show us your ID and explain why you are here."

The man fumbled in his back pocket, pulled out a black wallet, and it fell from his hand. The wallet bounced in front of Batiste. He bent to pick it up.

Batiste opened the wallet and stared into it. From my seat, I could see something shiny inside the wallet. Some kind of badge?

Batiste stared at it for a long moment, then returned his gaze to the killer. He studied the man for a moment. "You're a *vampire hunter*? Is this supposed to be real?"

The man nodded. "Yes. My badge. And my membership card . . . ohhhh . . ."

Batiste squinted at the open wallet again. "International Vampire Hunters? This card looks homemade."

"No. It's what I do. I . . ." In obvious pain, he pressed a hand to his forehead.

I jumped to my feet. "He's crazy. Don't listen to that. He killed my mother!"

Batiste motioned for me to sit down. Mrs. Hart took my arm and eased me back into the chair.

"My name . . . it's Cal . . . Calvin Imhoff," the man said. "I . . . I started the IVH."

"I—I don't believe this," Batiste said, frowning at the wallet.

"I've been trying to protect these kids," Imhoff said. He rubbed his head again. "I've been watching them, trying to warn them. Trying . . . trying to keep them safe."

"Safe?" Batiste said, standing over Imhoff. "Safe from what? From *you*? From a killer?"

Imhoff shut his eyes. When he opened them, he locked his gaze on Detective Batiste. "Let me tell you the bad news," he said. "You don't have a human killer. You have a vampire on your hands."

42

DEAR DIARY,

Wine gets better as it ages. That's what I've heard.

Ever since I was cheated and only got half of Winks's delicious nectar, I've had this gnawing hunger. It's as if drinking Winks's sweet blood only stirred my hunger instead of satisfying it.

Seeing Liam and Zane and my new girlfriends makes my mind spin, and it's all I can do to keep my truth from them. I have to work so hard not to let them inside.

I have to feed, Diary. The urge grows more powerful, more overwhelming every day. So tempting . . . So tempting . . . But I don't want to cause any more pain to my friends.

I feel so bad for Liam. He is crushed by the horror

of how he lost his mother. All of his personality seems to have been drained. What he saw when he found her on the kitchen floor lingers in his mind. He says the picture is there every time he closes his eyes, as if it's printed on his eyelids.

The funeral was unbearable. Liam and Jim, his father, sat and wept, sobbing loudly, so loud they nearly drowned out the minister. I felt so bad for them both.

And at the same time, my hunger made my whole body ache. I had to leave the funeral parlor before the service was over.

I can feed on a stranger, I decided. Maybe someone as old as Liam's mother. Someone not related to anyone, who wouldn't frighten my friends or bring them more sadness.

But blood isn't like wine. It doesn't grow sweeter and tastier as it ages. Blood goes sour and thin.

So unsatisfying.

Is there any greater disappointment than being unhappy with your meal?

But I couldn't help myself. One feed leads to another. One unsatisfying meal makes you desperate for the next one to be good.

I waited till the funeral ended. I watched from behind some shrubs across the street as people came

out, all of them grim-faced, some faces tear-stained.
People with their arms around each other's shoulders.
Some shaking their heads, standing in small groups,
talking quietly.

A picture of total grief. I felt so bad.

I watched the solemn pallbearers carry Mrs.
Franklin's coffin from the chapel and slide it into the
back of a long, black hearse.

I waited . . . waited for everyone to drive away. Waited
for the chapel doors to close. Then I crossed the street
and entered the building. I found the dark-suited funeral
director arranging the chairs in the now-silent chapel.

He was short and overweight, his belly pushing
against his white shirt. A red-faced man with a fringe of
short, black hair circling his round head.

Lots of blood. I could see it pulsing in veins at both
temples.

Old blood but I knew I couldn't be choosy.

He stood upright, surprise on his face, as I
approached. "Yes, miss? Can I help you?"

I nodded and spoke in a meek, little voice. "Did I
miss the cars to the cemetery?"

"Yes, I'm afraid you did."

I lowered my head. "Guess I'm too late."

"So sorry," he said. "They left about five minutes ago."

He bent down to pick some wadded-up Kleenex from the floor, and I jumped onto his back.

He uttered a grunt of surprise. I heard the air shoot out of his open mouth.

Riding his back, I forced him to the floor on his stomach. He hardly struggled. I think he went into instant shock.

I straddled him, keeping him down. Then I leaned forward, lowered my face to him, and punctured the back of his neck. The skin was taut, and it took a few bites to open him up.

Then I drank. The warm nectar flowed into my mouth, splashed over my face, and I drank sloppily. The blood wasn't sweet. Old blood. But I didn't care. I didn't care about anything but getting my fill.

I squeezed his neck with both hands, making the blood pump out faster. He was like a water fountain now. I sucked and slurped and practically bathed in it.

Sorry, sir, but at least you won't have to travel far for your funeral.

I always have strange thoughts when I'm feeding. I wonder if everyone does.

Ha. That's kind of a joke, isn't it, Diary?

Always leave them laughing. That's what I always say. Especially when I'm full.

43

LIAM NARRATES

After the funeral, Dad didn't invite any family members to come over. People understood he wanted to be alone. I found him in his bedroom, the bedroom he shared with Mom. He was sitting on the edge of the bed with his head down and his hands clasped in his lap.

I stopped at the doorway. I could see he was lost in thought. I didn't know if I should interrupt him or not.

It was like everything was awkward. Everything had changed. And I knew nothing would ever be the same.

There I was, standing in the doorway, unsure if I should speak to my own father. He suddenly looked so small, perched on the edge of the big queen-sized bed.

He raised his head and saw me. "Liam, hi. I was just . . ." His voice trailed off. He wasn't crying, but his eyes were red and watery.

"I didn't know . . . ," I started. "I didn't know if you wanted to . . . uh . . . hang out . . . or if you'd rather . . ."

"I just need to collect myself," he said. "There's a lot to be done now." He sighed. "Liam, maybe you should go work on your drone for a while. You know. Keep your hands busy. Maybe if you do something, it'll help take your mind off . . . off Mom."

I could feel myself choking up. "It . . . it's going to take a long time, Dad," I said. I spun away before I started to cry.

I made my way to the garage. It was a sunny afternoon. The air was still and dry. It felt more like summer than spring. I left the garage door open.

I could see Mom's petunia bed across the driveway. She had a thing about petunias, and kept that small flower garden in perfect shape. Dad always joked that her petunia obsession was one of the weirdest things about her.

I lowered the drone onto my worktable. I was still figuring out how to attach the video camera mount. It looked so clear and simple on the instruction sheet.

I wish Winks were here.

The thought flashed through my mind and made my chest tighten.

Winks would help cheer me up. He could always get *anyone* to laugh. Winks would help me get through this incredible sadness.

My best friend is dead. And my mother is dead.

I gripped the edge of the worktable. That was the first time it had occurred to me. The murders were of the people closest to me. They were the two people I cared about most.

What did this mean?

Was someone out to get me, to ruin my life? Were the murders actually about *me*?

Were the rest of my friends in danger? My father, too?

Was someone planning to murder *me*?

I gripped the table, these insane thoughts buzzing through my mind.

My best friend . . . My mother . . .

Imhoff, the vampire-hunter dude—the guy I put in the hospital . . . He said we have a vampire problem. I don't think anyone believed him. I know I didn't. If there was a vampire, it was him. I mean, what was he doing in the kitchen? And why did he try to run when he saw me step in?

After the funeral, someone told me Imhoff was in the hospital. They thought maybe I cracked his skull when I swung the big skillet at him. Or maybe he just had a very bad concussion.

I didn't want to think about him now. I hoped Batiste and the other cops would get the truth out of him.

I heard a noise from the driveway. I turned and saw Morgan walking up to the garage. Her red hair tossed behind her in the afternoon breeze. She didn't smile. I saw a square, white box in her hands.

"Hi, Liam." She stepped into the garage. "I brought you this. I . . . uh . . . well . . . I didn't know if you wanted visitors or not."

I took the box from her. "Sure. I guess," I said. "I . . . don't know what I want. I feel kind of numb, you know?"

She nodded. Her bright green eyes locked on mine. "So sorry."

I set the box on the worktable and started to lift the top.

"Some cupcakes," Morgan said. She shrugged. "I didn't know what to bring. I mean . . . what can you bring when someone's mother died?"

My throat tightened. I didn't want to cry in front of her. Even though she'd seen me cry and sob at the funeral.

"Are you working on your drone?" she asked.

I shook my head. "Not really."

Her eyes appeared to glow. I couldn't stop gazing

back at them. She didn't blink. I imagined an electrical current shooting from her eyes to mine.

The whole garage shimmered out of focus. I could see only her beautiful face and the glowing, electric eyes.

Was she hypnotizing me? Putting me in some kind of trance?

Crazy idea.

I picked up the long screwdriver I was using to attach the video camera mount. Was she saying something to me? I saw her lips move, but her voice seemed to come from far away.

I heard a billowing sound in my ears, like strong wind rustling inside my head. And still the eyes . . . those green eyes burned into my brain.

"Hey—!" The screwdriver slipped from my hand. I cried out as the sharp tip scraped my wrist. The screwdriver bounced soundlessly to the concrete floor.

All I could hear was the roar in my head.

I glanced down. I saw a trickle of red blood seep from a line in my wrist. It spread quickly over my skin.

Morgan grabbed my hand. She raised it close to her face. "Oh, Liam. You cut yourself." Her voice broke through the roaring wind in my ears.

"It's okay," I murmured.

I watched her lower her face to my wrist. And I felt

her tongue on my skin as she licked at the trickle of blood.

Her hair fell over her head, hiding her face from me. She licked again. "Tastes like your mother."

That's what I thought she said.

But that was *impossible*.

"What did you say?" I pulled my arm away, trying to break the spell, trying to stop the whirlwind in my head. "I didn't hear right, Morgan. What did you just say?"

"I said we need to get you a Band-Aid."

"Oh. Yeah. I see." The garage came back into focus. Her eyes caught the light from the lowering sun outside the garage and appeared to twinkle.

She wiped the blood off my wrist with one finger. Then she dipped the finger into her mouth.

I narrowed my eyes at her. *Is she crazy? Why did she do that?*

44

LIAM CONTINUES

The rest of the day passed slowly. Dad and I ate a silent dinner. I don't even remember what we had. Our cousins had sent over a big casserole, some kind of noodle thing. Dad served it without even warming it up.

The whole time, I stared at Mom's empty chair and fought back the urge to cry. My cut wrist was bandaged, and it throbbed a little. Dad asked if I thought it needed stitches. But I told him it wasn't a deep cut at all.

"How could you cut yourself with a screwdriver?" he asked.

I shrugged. "I'm not really sure."

What happened in the garage that afternoon wasn't clear to me. As if a fog had settled over everything.

But I remembered how strange Morgan had acted

when my wrist started to bleed. It kept troubling my mind, and I had a growing urge to tell someone.

Zane wasn't home. After dinner, I drove over to Julie's house. I found her in the dining room. She and Amber and Delia were seated around the dining room table, a pile of cards and envelopes between them.

As I walked in, they raised their eyes, and their faces twisted in concern. Julie stood up, walked over, and hugged me. "How are you doing, Liam?"

"Are you okay?" Amber asked.

"Did you have dinner? We have some pizza left over," Julie said, motioning to the kitchen.

"We didn't expect to see you," Delia said. "I mean, so soon after . . ."

"I'm trying to deal with everything," I told them. "It's been a tough day."

I glanced at the envelopes stacked on the table. "What are you doing?"

"Sending out invitations to the alumni carnival," Julie said. "Want to help us?" She walked back to her chair.

"Not really," I said. "I . . . want to tell you guys something."

"Have you heard from the police?" Delia asked, setting down the card she was working on.

"It's not about that," I said. "It's about Morgan."

That got their attention. All eyes were on me now.

"I saw Morgan at your mom's funeral," Amber said. "She sat in the back and kept her head down the whole time."

"I saw her, too," Delia said. "When it was over, I went over to talk to her, but she hurried away. I don't know if she saw me or not."

Amber pushed her glasses up on her nose. "She looked as pale as milk," she said. "Like she was sick. Poor Morgan. She was so totally devastated after Winks was murdered. And now to have a second murder . . ." She gasped. "Oh. Sorry, Liam."

I dropped down on the edge of the chair next to hers. "Are you going to let me tell you my story, or not?"

All three grew silent and turned their gaze on me.

"Morgan came to my house," I said. "After the funeral. She said she was feeling weird, out of sorts."

Julie narrowed her eyes at me. "So she just dropped by your house?"

I nodded. "She was being nice. She brought me some cupcakes."

"What flavor?" Amber asked.

"Shut up, Amber," Julie snapped. "That's not funny."

"Just asking," Amber replied.

"So what happened?" Delia asked.

"I was in the garage. Dad thought it might help me get through the day if I worked on building my drone. But I couldn't really concentrate on it. I couldn't concentrate on anything. Like I had clouds in my brain."

"And Morgan showed up?" Julie said.

"Yes. But here's what I wanted to tell you." I leaned over the table and lowered my voice. "I dropped a screwdriver. It slipped out of my hand, and the tip scraped my wrist."

I held up my bandaged wrist.

"Was it a bad cut?" Julie asked.

"No," I said. "But it started to bleed. Just a little. And Morgan took my hand. I thought she wanted to inspect the cut. But no. She raised my hand to her mouth and started to lick off the blood."

Delia gasped. Amber and Julie just stared.

"You think Morgan is a *vampire*?" Delia said.

"I'm just saying—" I started.

"No. No, no, no, that doesn't make sense," Julie insisted.

"Morgan held my hand to her mouth and licked it up. And—"

"Morgan is a total flirt," Amber said. "She's not a vampire."

"She was coming on to you, Liam," Julie said.

"If Morgan is a vampire, I am, too," Delia said.

"They caught the killer, Liam," Julie said. "That weird guy who thinks he's a vampire hunter. We can relax now. They've got him."

"Okay, okay." I raised my hands to signal an end to the discussion. "I'm only telling you what happened. I—"

A sound behind me made me turn around.

Morgan came hurrying in, her hair fluttering behind her. "Sorry I'm late. Are all the envelopes addressed?"

"No. Plenty more to do," Julie said. "Where were you?"

Morgan flung her jacket onto an empty chair. "I was at the blood bank. Did you know they have takeout?"

45

MORGAN NARRATES

Oh, wow. The looks on their faces—priceless!

Amber's eyes bulged behind those thick glasses. I thought Delia was going to fall off her chair. Julie only blinked. She's the smartest one in the room.

I laughed. "I was in your front room," I said. "I heard everything Liam said."

His face was as red as fire, and he made a choking sound. Poor guy. I've never seen anyone look that embarrassed. He jumped to his feet. He opened his mouth to speak, but no sound came out. He gave me a pleading look.

I walked over and gave his chest a playful, two-handed push. "Liam, do you really think I'm a vampire?" I snapped my teeth at his neck a couple of times.

The girls laughed. Liam backed away, his face even darker.

"I . . . wasn't serious," he said. "It was like a joke."

I didn't let him off the hook. "What's the joke part?"

He decided to play the sympathy card. "Look, Morgan, I've had a bad day, you know? My mother's funeral? Maybe I'm not thinking clearly. Maybe . . ."

I should just bite his throat and drain him dry, I thought, watching him squirm. He looked so cute. *I should drain him right in front of everyone. That would give the girls a thrill.*

The thought made me burst out laughing. I was seriously tempted.

Too bad I'm still so full . . . from his mother.

"Give Liam a break," Julie said. She motioned to a dining room chair across the table from her. "Come sit down, Morgan. I want to show you all something."

I could see she was eager to change the subject. She could see Liam was suffering. I patted his hand. "You're forgiven," I murmured.

Julie hurried from the room as I took my place next to Delia at the table. "Still lots of invitations to address," she said.

Liam sat down, too. His face started to return to its normal color. Amber was squinting at me through her glasses, studying me. I couldn't tell what she was thinking.

"Look what we've got," Julie said, striding back into the room. She raised a long-handled ax in one hand. The handle was painted in blue and yellow stripes.

"Are you practicing to be a lumberjack?" Liam said. It wasn't funny, but at least he was trying.

"It's the official Linden Vikings ax," Julie said, holding it high. "See? The yellow and blue stripes, the team colors?"

"We get it," Amber said. "But . . . why do we need an ax?"

"It's from the old days," Julie replied. "They used this ax to chop down the goalposts after winning a state championship. You know. A ceremony. The ax has been passed down for over fifty years."

"And why do you have it?" Amber asked.

"Each year, it's given to a Linden graduate who comes to the carnival to keep for a year. It's an honor, see."

"Can I hold it?" Liam jumped to his feet. He reached out both hands.

"Careful," Julie said. "The blade is as sharp as it looks."

Liam raised the ax and held it for a while. Then his expression changed. His face appeared to crumble. His body slumped. "Wish . . . ," he muttered. "Wish I could use this on that guy who killed my mother."

Then he burst out sobbing. Julie took the ax from him. Liam covered his face with both hands. His shoulders rolled up and down as his loud sobs shook his entire body.

Julie turned and carried the ax from the room. Amber and Delia jumped up and wrapped Liam in a hug. They held on to him until his body stopped shaking and the sobs faded to silent tears.

"Can we drive you home?" Amber asked.

Liam shook his head. He took a Kleenex from Delia and wiped his eyes and cheeks. "No. I'm okay now. I can drive myself."

He started toward the front door. I took his arm and helped steady him, and we walked to his car. I opened the car door for him.

"Sorry . . . about before," he said, avoiding my eyes.

"Forget about it," I said. "At your house this afternoon, I didn't mean to upset you." I leaned over and kissed his cheek. "I like you."

I couldn't see his face. He didn't reply. Just closed the car door, started it up, and squealed away.

As I walked back to the house, I thought about Liam. *He's tense and sad now. His blood will taste sour.*

Liam is off the hook . . . at least for a while.

His buddy Zane would taste sweeter, like a fine dessert.

Yes. Zane. Zane the comedian who is always serious. The sweetest!

My mouth is already watering. Zane for dessert.

When I stepped back into the dining room, the girls had returned to the stack of envelopes. "Poor Liam," I murmured. "I hope I didn't upset him with my vampire joke. I'm so sorry about it now. It wasn't in good taste, *was* it?"

"Don't feel bad," Julie said. "Liam and his mother were very close. I know he always felt closer to her than to his dad."

Delia shivered. "Two murders in Linden. Two people we knew. I am so freaking out. I am seriously scared."

Julie's phone buzzed. She raised it to her ear. "Hi, Mom. Where are you?"

I could hear Mrs. Hart's voice on the other end.

Julie's mouth dropped open. "Oh no." A moan escaped her throat.

"What is it?" Amber cried.

Julie's mom talked some more. Julie just kept repeating, "Oh no, oh no."

Finally, she clicked off and set the phone facedown

on the table. She shook her head.

"What is it? What did she say?" Amber demanded.

"Remember the funeral director today? That chubby guy in the tight suit? He did the ceremony at the funeral for Liam's mom?"

We all nodded.

"He seemed nice," I said.

"He—he was murdered, too," Julie said, her voice cracking on the words. "They just found him. In the chapel. He was killed. They think some time after the funeral ceremony."

Silence for a long moment. Everyone was trying to take in the shocking news.

"Who would *do* that?" I cried finally. "That's horrible!"

"This means the killer is still out there," Julie whispered.

Everyone stared at one another.

"Is someone just killing people we know?" Amber cried, her voice cracking. "Is someone following us around and randomly killing us?"

No one had an answer.

Julie sighed. "What should we do?"

"Let's keep working," I said. "We can talk and maybe take our minds off what's happening."

"Yes. We've got to keep busy," Delia said. "It's the only way."

We took our places, and Julie passed around envelopes and invitations.

I volunteered for the invitation-sending committee because I had a good reason. I had some surprises in store for all my new friends.

I had some people *I* wanted to invite. Special people.

"Do you have any extras?" I asked Julie. "I just thought of some people I need to invite to the carnival."

46

JULIE NARRATES

"Are you sure I'm doing the right thing? I can't decide. I keep going back and forth."

Zane paced my living room, hands stuffed into his jeans pockets, shaking his head. His dark eyes appeared to be pleading with me.

As if I had any answers.

"I can't tell you whether to go ahead with your stand-up act tonight," I said. I motioned for him to join me on the couch. But he ignored my signals and kept pacing back and forth. "You're wearing a hole in the carpet, Zane."

"I can't sit still. I feel as if my head is exploding." He swept a hand tensely back through his short, dark hair. "How can I be funny if I'm so wound up?"

"Then don't do it," I said.

He blinked at me in surprise.

He looked so cute when he was so tightly wired. I couldn't help it. I knew he was upset. But I just wanted to grab him and hug him and kiss him until we both felt better.

We all missed Winks, but I think Zane was having the hardest time accepting his death. Zane has always been so sensitive and thoughtful. He thinks a lot about things, sometimes too much. I mean, it's hard for him to let things go.

I think we were ten or eleven when his dog was hit by a car. Zane took it so hard. I remember him crying and carrying on. It was like he didn't know who to blame. He didn't come out of his room for days.

Of course, having Winks as a friend was even more important to him than the dog. He was too old to shut himself up in his room now. But I could see he had the same sadness and the same disbelief, and the same anxiety as when we were ten.

"I just don't know if I can be funny," Zane said, lowering his head. "I feel like my timing will be totally off. Last time we were all there, Winks was right across from the stage, grinning up at me. I can still see his goofy grin.

It meant a lot to me, especially since no one was laughing very much."

"Well, okay. Your cousin will understand if you cancel," I said.

"Yeah. Martin's a good guy. But it's like a really big favor. You know. To let me go up there on open mic night. He might decide . . ." His voice trailed off.

I patted the couch cushion beside me. "Come sit down. You're making me crazy with your pacing."

"I don't have any new jokes," Zane said. "How could I have new jokes?" He slumped beside me and crossed his arms in front of his T-shirt.

"Do you want to write some tonight?" I said. "We could try together."

He thought about it for a long moment. "Yeah. Maybe."

I couldn't hold back any longer. How long had I been trying to get Zane's attention? Years? Why had I been so shy with him? Just because we'd known each other forever?

My heart started to flutter in my chest. "I want to tell you something," I said softly.

He turned toward me. "What?"

I lurched forward, threw my arms around his

shoulders, and kissed him. I moved my lips against his. I was desperate to show him I was serious about this.

He uttered a little cry of surprise. I could feel him start to pull back. But then he got into it. I guess he surrendered to it.

Did he want this, too? Did he have the same feelings I had?

I hoped so.

We were both breathless when the kiss ended. I pressed my forehead against his.

He snickered. "Is that what you wanted to tell me?"

"Yes."

"Well, can I tell *you* something?"

I nodded.

And he kissed me again.

I raised my hands to the back of his neck and held him there.

Zane and I have wasted a lot of time, I thought.

But that's old news now.

Then the front doorbell rang.

I slid my hands off his neck and ended the kiss. Zane jumped to his feet.

A few seconds later, I opened the door, and gasped. The vampire hunter was standing there. He had a bandage covering his white-blond hair. He wore a long, tan trench coat despite the warm spring air.

He raised his wallet with the fake ID. I read his name: Calvin Imhoff. He shook his head, his expression grim.

I uttered a cry. "Oh no. Has there been another murder?"

47

ZANE NARRATES

Saturday morning, I kept waking up every hour on the hour. But I pulled the bedspread over my head, curled up tight, and kept forcing myself to go back to sleep.

Every time I woke up, I thought about Julie. In the back of my mind, I'd always suspected she and I would end up together. I guess the reason I never did anything about it was that I just accepted that one day it would happen.

Does that make sense?

Nothing was making sense in my jumbled-up brain.

At eleven, my phone ringtone made me sit up, instantly alert. I grabbed the phone off the bedside table and, blinking away any lingering sleepiness, gazed at the screen.

"Morgan?"

"Hey, Zane. How you doing?"

I stifled a yawn and, sitting on the edge of the bed, stretched my back. "Not bad."

Why is Morgan calling me on a Saturday morning?

"I just wanted to say I'm sorry I missed your stand-up act last night," she said. "How'd it go?"

"It didn't," I replied. "I canceled it."

"You didn't do it?"

"I couldn't," I said. "I don't feel funny. I . . . couldn't write any new jokes, and . . . I just knew it was too soon. You know."

"Yeah, I know," she said. "No one feels funny. How could you? With someone killing people you know."

"That weird Imhoff guy showed up last night," I said. "At Julie's."

"You were at Julie's?"

Do I hear a tiny bit of jealousy in Morgan's voice? Is she interested in me now . . . now that Winks is gone?

I pictured her face. So awesomely beautiful. So perfect.

And then I thought about Julie. Julie and me, together now as we should be.

Morgan . . . Julie . . .

"Imhoff was all bandaged and weird because of Liam

smashing that skillet into his face," I said.

"Why did the police let him go? He's the murderer, right?"

"I . . . I don't know. I don't understand—"

"Well, what did he want?" Morgan's voice suddenly sounded sharp. Suspicious.

"At first we thought he'd come to tell us about another murder. But we were wrong. He just wanted information. About the murder that happened while he was in custody. I mean, he asked us a bunch of questions."

"Like what?"

"Like did we see anything? Did we hear anything? Did we hear any rumors at school? Did we have any hunches about who did the murders?"

Morgan snickered. "Hunches? You mean he was desperate?"

"Yeah. Desperate," I said. "I don't think he has a clue."

A pause. Then she said, "He can't be a real vampire hunter, can he?"

"Maybe he is," I replied. "He seemed totally serious about it. He said he's going around asking everyone if they have any idea at all."

"Why does he think it's someone at school?" Morgan demanded. "It's probably a stranger, right? Probably someone no one knows."

I had to think about that. "Yeah. Maybe."

"I mean, we don't have a vampire walking around in the halls at Linden High, do we?" Morgan laughed again. "That's ridiculous."

"Well . . ."

"This crazy dude is wasting his time questioning us," Morgan said, becoming more heated. "If there really is a vampire, shouldn't he be able to get the vampire's DNA from the victims' bodies?"

"You've been watching too many *Forensic Files*," I said. I could hear my parents arguing about something downstairs. Maybe they were upset that I was sleeping so late.

I glanced at the clock. So, okay. I slept through my tennis lesson. But what's the big deal?

"Actually, he asked about *you*," I said.

"Huh? Me? What about me?"

"He asked if we knew anything about you. Like where you came from and where you used to go to school. And how long did you know Winks. And did you know Liam's mother. He had a bunch of questions about you, Morgan."

She laughed. "Now we *know* he's totally clueless. I'm not a vampire, Zane. I'm a werewolf."

We both laughed.

"But only under the full moon," Morgan added. "Next time you see Imhoff, you should tell him that."

We both laughed some more. "I'd better go," I said.

"Zane, can I ask you a favor?" Morgan said.

So this is why she called?

"I have a bunch of stuff I have to bring up from the basement," she said, "and I'm all alone here. Think you could come help me?"

She said it kind of teasingly. I mean, she actually made it sound sexy.

Could anyone resist that beautiful face?

She is so totally hot.

"Yeah. Sure," I said. "Let me grab some breakfast, and I'll come over in an hour or so."

"Oh, thank you, Zane. You're a real sweetheart."

Sweetheart?

I pulled on a pair of long cargo shorts and a gray T-shirt, and made my way downstairs. Mom and Dad were just on their way out to go grocery shopping.

"We thought you were going to sleep all day," Dad said.

"How are you feeling?" Mom's eyes studied me up and down. "Those shorts are too wrinkled to wear outside."

"I'll unwrinkle them," I said. "I'm feeling a little better."

Dad studied me, too. "You didn't do your stand-up thing last night?"

I shook my head. "I called Martin. He totally understood."

Mom nodded sympathetically. "It'll take time, Zane. Just give it time."

Dad pushed open the screen door. "Anything we can get you to cheer you up?"

I thought hard. "Just the usual."

The door closed behind them. A few seconds later, I heard their car start up.

I grabbed a bowl of cornflakes and a glass of apple juice. Then I checked out my shorts in the mirror. They looked okay to me.

I hurried over to Morgan's house. I think she'd been waiting for me because she greeted me at the front door as I walked up her front lawn.

She wore a sleeveless blue tee over red short-shorts. Her hair was tied behind her head in a single ponytail. She looked so amazing, my breath caught in my throat. I actually stopped breathing for a second!

"Hey, thanks for coming," she called. She came

running down the lawn, ponytail bouncing behind her, those green eyes shining in the midday sunlight, and gave me a hug.

The hug lasted longer than a normal hug. I mean, it wasn't just a hug of greeting. She took my hand and, clasping it hard, led me into the front entryway of her house.

"So you've got stuff in your basement?" I said. My voice sounded muffled, kind of breathless. I was, like, under her spell. She was too awesome to be real.

"We're just moving in," she said, still holding my hand. "There's a lot of cleaning out to do."

"Well, lead the way," I said.

But she didn't lead the way; instead, she backed me up against the entryway wall. She pushed me gently with both hands. Then she slid her hands around my waist, brought her face close to mine, and kissed me.

Her lips pushed hard against mine, so hard it hurt. She kept her eyes wide-open. They burned into mine as her mouth pressed against me.

Her hands gripped me tightly. My heart was pounding so hard, I felt as if I had a bird in my chest, fluttering its wings to get out.

Fluttering . . . Fluttering . . .

I knew I was in some kind of fog . . . a white mist

that circled me . . . something unreal that played with my mind. Her lips were real. Her kiss was real. But I felt myself falling into a silent whirlwind.

And then she raised her head. Her mouth opened wide. Her eyes glowed like green fire.

"I can't hold back any longer."

That's what I think she said. I felt close to her and far away at the same time. No way to catch my balance. I stared into the bright mist, waiting for her lips again.

"I can't hold back any longer."

I didn't get her lips. I got her teeth. I saw them pull up, long white teeth. She gripped me by the shoulders and pressed me against the wall.

She lowered her head, eyes glowing, mouth open hungrily.

Was I imagining it? Her face began to change. Her cheeks appeared to sag. Her whole face appeared to melt, her eyes sinking deep into their sockets.

Nooooo. I am hallucinating. This is crazy. This isn't happening.

Then I felt her teeth . . . felt them slide against my neck . . . tickling . . . tickling . . . just before she plunged them into my throat.

48

MORGAN NARRATES

My whole body trembled at the thought of this sweet meal. My skin tingled as if electricity coursed over me. The animal hunger I felt would soon give way to a feeling of warm ecstasy as I fed on Zane.

I teased him, tickling the skin on his throat with my teeth. My saliva ran onto his neck. Yes, I was drooling. Liam's mother had been filling but oh so unsatisfying.

And now . . . I prepared my feast. Held him carefully in place. Fogged his brain so that he would willingly sacrifice, willingly give of himself, give me *life*!

"Hey, Morgan—*here* you are!"

The voice startled me so badly, I uttered a shriek.

I jerked my head back, pulled my teeth from Zane's

throat. I hadn't even punctured the skin.

Struggling to regain my composure, I kept my back turned until my face returned to normal. Then I saw Delia stride into the room. She dangled car keys in one hand. "Your door was open," she said, "so I—"

She stopped and her mouth dropped open when she saw my embrace of Zane. "Oh. Sorry. Did I interrupt?"

"Uh . . . no," I said, taking a step back, removing my hands from his chest. "I was giving Zane a shoulder massage. He's totally tense."

"Who isn't?" Delia replied, crossing the room to us. "How's it going, Zane?"

Zane blinked his eyes a few times. He flashed Delia a smile. I could see the confusion on his face. He was completely dazed. I knew he didn't remember a thing.

Delia waved her car keys. "I'm just on my way to school. To help Julie and the others finish decorating the gym for the alumni carnival. I thought maybe you'd like to come pitch in."

"Yeah. Sure. Of course, I do," I said.

I realized I was holding my stomach. The gnawing feeling inside me was so intense. Could she and Zane hear my stomach growl?

I was so close, I thought. *So close.*

Then Delia ruined my meal.

Well, now I have reason to pay you back, Delia dear. I never noticed what a pretty throat you have.

Well, I had *many* surprises planned for the alumni party. And now, I'd definitely have one for Delia.

49

JULIE NARRATES

"Has anybody seen Delia?" I asked. "She promised to come and help with the posters."

"I think she stopped to pick up Morgan," Amber answered. She was on a tall ladder against the gym wall, tacking up the *Beavis and Butt-Head* poster.

I had about twenty helpers now, one day before the party, and the gym was looking like a nineties time warp. The long wall was nearly covered in posters and big color photos of all the shows and stars our nineties' alumni watched.

We had *Saved by the Bell* and *Fresh Prince* and *Ren & Stimpy* and *Full House* posters. Caleb Farr, whose father worked at an ad agency in New York City during the nineties, gave us life-sized cutouts of the Power

Rangers and Teenage Mutant Ninja Turtles.

My favorite poster showed a great action scene from *Buffy the Vampire Slayer*. I love that show. I watch the old episodes all the time on Netflix.

Amber finished tacking up the *Beavis and Butt-Head* poster. She climbed down the ladder and stepped up beside me to admire the poster gallery. She had beads of sweat glistening on her forehead. We had all been working really hard.

"My parents watched a show called *Rugrats*," she said. "I don't think it was about rats. They said it was *huge*. Everyone watched it."

"I couldn't find a *Rugrats* poster," I said. "But I think we did pretty well."

"Who is working on the music mix?" Amber asked.

"You know. Frankie Gerard. Mr. Tech. He told me he's doing a two-hour jam. Mostly disco stuff."

"Cool," Amber said. "My cousin is seriously into nineties disco. Like the songs they play at basketball games during time-outs? 'Pump Up the Jam' . . . 'Whoomp! (There It Is).'" I love that one.

"We have to test the sound system," I said. "Make sure we can get it loud enough." I sighed. "There's still a lot to do."

A loud crash made me jump.

I turned to see that the helium tank had fallen over. Some kids were hoisting it back up. We needed the helium to blow up the balloons. Something else that was on my list.

"Can I have everyone's attention?" a voice boomed.

Calvin Imhoff, the so-called vampire hunter, strode into the gym. The doors closed loudly behind him. He had a bandage around the top of his head, dark glasses over his eyes. Even at a distance, I could see that his face was red and swollen.

He wore a black suit, white shirt open at the neck. He walked steadily to the center of the gym, eyes straight forward, not glancing at our poster-covered walls. He waved both arms, summoning everyone to gather around him.

Kids muttered and questioned each other. A lot of them had never seen Imhoff before and had no idea who he was. Amber and I hesitated, exchanging glances. *What is he doing here? Why is he interrupting our work? Should we call the police?*

It took Imhoff a while to get everyone quiet. He stood stiffly, facing everyone, hands jammed into his pants pockets. The high ceiling lights reflected off his sunglasses, filling the glass with silver so we couldn't see his eyes.

"For those of you who haven't met me, I'm Calvin Imhoff. I hunt vampires," he started. He held up his badge.

"I saw a badge like that on eBay," a boy shouted from the back of the crowd of kids. "Did you get a whistle, too?"

A few kids laughed.

Imhoff's whole body stiffened. He bit his bottom lip. "I don't think we want to make jokes when there's a killer on the loose," he said.

"I don't think you want to be in here," I told him. "I'm calling an administrator."

"All of your lives are at risk!" he shouted.

Silence now. The only sound was the loud hum of the air-conditioning vents at the top of the gym. A poster hadn't been tacked up right and made a flapping sound on the wall behind us.

"I want you to all be safe for your alumni carnival," Imhoff continued. He scratched at the bottom of his bandage. "Some of my colleagues will be on duty. I want to assure you that we will take precautions and will be alert to any problem that might arise."

I narrowed my eyes at Imhoff. Liam still thought he was the killer. But the police let him go. That had to mean they had somehow ruled him out. That it wasn't him.

My mind whirred with questions. I thought about Winks. It was hard not to think about Winks.

"You mean, you think the killer may come to the carnival?" I asked.

Imhoff scratched at his bandage. "I'm just saying that we will be ready." He shook his head bitterly. "I've failed so far. When I came to Linden, my assignment was to keep everyone safe. I've failed."

He stood silent for a long moment. He pulled off his sunglasses and rubbed the bridge of his nose. His silvery eyes gazed down the line of kids.

"I knew who it was, and I couldn't do anything about it," he said. He twirled the sunglasses tensely in his hand. "I knew who it was. The vampire. That's the specialty of my fellow workers, you know. We know who they are."

I saw some kids shift uneasily. I heard some mumbles, and a few kids rolled their eyes.

I didn't blame them. Imhoff seemed to be talking to himself, not to us. And what he was saying was strange. I couldn't figure out why he was telling us all this.

"Sure, we try to keep it quiet. Isn't there enough bad news? Enough problems to panic over?" he continued.

He didn't notice that people were getting restless, eager to get back to their decorating chores and preparations.

Imhoff's eyes darted from side to side. He slid the sunglasses back over them. "I knew who it was when I came here," he repeated. "I tried to warn off that boy Winkleman. I tried to scare him away from her."

He shook his head. He definitely was talking to himself now. He was looking down, shaking his head, rubbing the bandage over his hair. "I failed. I tried to scare him. I was too late. I knew her. I knew who the vampire was."

His voice was strained now. His chest was heaving with each breath.

"I knew . . . I knew her . . . I knew . . . But I couldn't . . ."

His knees appeared to fold. He started to fall. A whistling sound escaped his mouth, like air seeping out of a balloon.

Startled, I rushed forward and grabbed his arm to help him stay on his feet. "Are you okay?" I asked.

He nodded. "Yes. Okay. I'm okay."

"Who is the vampire?" someone shouted.

"You know who it is? Tell us!"

Imhoff leaned heavily on me. I could see he was falling. He couldn't support himself.

"Who is it?" Another voice from the crowd.

"I'll . . . tell . . . you . . . ," Imhoff said, his voice weak, failing. "It's . . ."

A hush fell over the gym. Imhoff dropped to his knees. "It's the girl who calls herself Morgan Marks."

Then he passed out.

I tried to hold him up, but he toppled forward, hitting his head on the gym floor. He didn't move.

"Somebody call 911!" I cried.

"Morgan Marks?" Liam appeared from the crowd of kids. Had he been there all along?

"Morgan Marks?" he repeated. "If she's a vampire, I'm a Hobbit!"

Some kids laughed.

A guy named Kerry Smithson tapped knuckles with Liam. "If she's a vampire, I'm a Wookiee!"

"Morgan Marks? He's seriously nuts."

"If she's a vampire, I'm the Tooth Fairy!"

"This dude was out of his head," a boy named Carlos Fuentes said. "Like he was dazed or something. He was totally in la-la land. He didn't know what he was saying."

"It's my bad," Liam said. "I slammed his head twice with a skillet."

"Shut up! Shut up! Stop talking, everyone!" Amber

cried. "Don't you see? He's unconscious. Did anyone call for help?"

"The ambulance is on the way," Kerry Smithson said, holding up his iPhone.

I heard a banging at the gym doors. "That must be the medics," I said.

The doors swung open and Delia came walking in, a smile on her face. "Hi, guys. Sorry I'm late," she called. "But look who I brought with me to help out."

I couldn't help myself. I let out a sharp cry as Morgan Marks followed her into the gym.

50

JULIE CONTINUES

No one said a word. We all watched the two girls make their way across the gym. On the floor, Imhoff let out a groan. One of his legs twitched, but he didn't open his eyes.

"What happened?" Delia cried, spotting his crumpled body. "Who *is* that?" She started to run toward him. Morgan followed, blinking, her face twisted in confusion.

"It's the vampire hunter," Liam said, stepping forward to greet them. "I think it's his head injury. The one I gave him. He just . . . collapsed."

I watched Morgan and thought about Imhoff's accusation. She raised both hands to her face as she gazed down at his unmoving body. "Is he . . . breathing?"

Before anyone could answer, two green-uniformed medics came bursting into the gym, carrying a bag of equipment. We all stepped out of their way as they trotted up to us. One of them knelt beside Imhoff and reached for his wrist to check his pulse.

"What happened here?" the other medic asked.

"He fainted," I said. "As you can see, he has a head injury."

"He was in the hospital," Amber added. "Maybe he came out too soon."

It didn't take them long to get Imhoff onto a stretcher. He raised his head and gazed around as they started to carry him away. One of the medics put a hand on his chest and made him lie back down.

As soon as they were out of sight, everyone started talking at once. I kept my eyes on Morgan, thinking about what Imhoff had said. Even with her hair tied back loosely, some of it falling over her face, and no makeup at all, and in ragged jeans and a baggy T-shirt, she looked beautiful. She didn't look like a vampire.

But what does a vampire look like?

I felt a chill at the back of my neck. What if Imhoff *wasn't* out of his head? What if he wasn't just talking crazy because of his injury?

I'd heard rumors that Winks had been drained of his

blood. And some people said that the same thing had happened to Liam's mother.

A real vampire in Linden? It didn't seem possible. And it definitely didn't seem possible that Morgan Marks could be the vampire. For one thing, she was too light, too thin. How could she drink that much blood?

Crazy thoughts. I shut my eyes and tried to get my head together. We still had a lot of work to prepare for the party.

I opened my eyes when Delia grabbed my wrist. "Julie, what was he doing here?" she demanded.

"He came to warn us," Liam spoke up before I could. He answered Delia's question but his eyes were on Morgan. "He said the killer is still out there somewhere. He said he'd keep us safe."

"But then he fainted to the floor," I added.

"Horrible," Morgan murmured. She still had her hands covering her cheeks. "How horrible. Everyone must have freaked."

"It was kind of frightening," I said. I was dying to tell Morgan that Imhoff had accused her. But I just couldn't say the words.

To my surprise, Liam said them for me. "Imhoff was muttering to himself. He kept repeating things," he told her. "It was crazy. He said that *you* are the vampire. He said he came to Linden to protect us from you, and he failed."

Liam watched Morgan to see how she would react. So did I. So did everyone.

Her hands slid from her cheeks. Her mouth dropped open in surprise, and I could see her thinking hard, her green eyes on Liam.

"Of *course*, I'm a vampire," she said. "Look at my fangs." She opened her mouth and clicked her teeth a few times. She laughed. "Don't I *look* like a vampire?"

"Not exactly," Liam said.

She smiled at him. "Thanks. I guess that's a compliment."

Kids shifted uncomfortably. A few muttered to each other, keeping their voices low.

Morgan turned to me. "Julie knows I'm a vampire. Right, Julie? You work in the office with your mother. You saw my old school records. You know I went to Transylvania Middle School."

Some kids laughed.

Morgan was getting her point across. The idea of her being a vampire was a total joke.

But then I remembered something. "Morgan, actually, we *don't* have your school records. They never came. Your file is totally empty. So . . . maybe you *did* go to Transylvania Middle School."

She grinned at me. "Maybe I did."

Amber tugged down the sleeves of her white sweat-shirt. She cleared her throat. Her eyes were on Morgan. "We all feel weird and frightened and tense," she said, "because of the horrible murders. But we have to try to have a normal life and just keep on. You know. Keep on keeping on."

She took a breath. She didn't usually speak up in a crowd. I could see it made her nervous. "And we can't start accusing people we know of being vampires. That's just crazy."

"She's right," Delia chimed in. "We can't accuse one another. We don't know anything about that Imhoff guy. He may be a total nutjob. If he came here to protect us, why didn't he save Winks's life? Why didn't he save *any-one's* life?"

"Yes, he's a nutjob," Liam said. "Did anyone check up on him? Did the police check? Did they just let him go free?"

Again, voices rang out. Everyone had an opinion about Imhoff.

He had to be crazy. Just take one look at Morgan. She's beautiful. And normal. And funny.

But then another chill tightened the back of my neck

as I remembered the letter from her old school. The letter that said she had died five years ago.

I froze watching her, listening to everyone putting Imhoff down, talking about his crazy speech to us. *Out of his head. He's out of his head.*

I froze watching Morgan and remembered snapping the photos of her in my mother's office with my phone. The photos that turned out to be blank, a blur. No school records. No photos. And that letter that said she had died. The letter she explained as a mix-up.

I had to get everyone back to work. I didn't have time for these thoughts. I didn't have time . . .

But what if? What if?

What if Imhoff was telling the truth?

Would someone else die because we didn't believe him?

51

JULIE CONTINUES

It rained the day of the alumni carnival, and I stood at our living room window, staring into the glare of the gray and glumly watching the big raindrops splash over our front yard.

I felt Mom's hands on my shoulders. "You can't control the weather, Julie," she said softly. "You've controlled everything else wonderfully. You've done a great job for this party."

"There's been so much bad news," I said. "I just want something to be nice. And normal."

"I'm sure it will be," Mom said. "I'm so impressed with your organizing skills. You never could organize your clothes closet, and now you organized this whole event."

I rolled my eyes. "Thanks for the compliment, Mom."

Amber and Delia showed up at the gym to check over the last details. A couple of the posters had come down and we tacked them back up. A few balloons had to be reinflated.

Frankie Gerard came to test the sound system. The three of us clapped our hands to our ears as "Ice Ice Baby" blasted from the speakers. Frankie shouted something to us, but we couldn't hear him. Finally, he stopped the music.

"Frankie, we couldn't hear you," I called.

"I was asking if that was loud enough," he shouted.

"I think maybe some people would like to have a conversation," Amber said.

Frankie squinted at us. "You mean turn it down?"

"Where are the party bags?" Delia asked. "Did anyone fill them up?"

The party bags were a going-away gift, a collection of nineties candies in each bag. "They should be in the hall," I said. "I'll go with you."

The red-and-yellow bags were lined up against one wall. I peeked inside one. It had Skittles, Hubba Bubba Bubble Tape, Sour Patch Kids, Haribo Goldbears, Airheads, Nerds, and Wonka Runts. Excellent.

Delia held up a pack of Sour Patch Kids. "Are these really sour?"

I shrugged. "Probably."

A hundred candy bags all lined up looked impressive. Some of the candy had been hard to find. But we wanted to bring back memories for the alums. And we expected one hundred guests at the carnival.

Sure enough, people started to arrive a little after seven. I could feel my muscles tighten as the first couple walked in. I told myself to lighten up. Everything was organized. The party *had* to be a total success.

You don't have to do everything, Julie, I told myself for the hundredth time. *Everyone has a job. Everyone is in place.*

I gazed around the gym. Frankie had his music going, toned down so it didn't seem to be coming from *inside* your brain. Liam and Delia were at the food table. Amber was at the bar.

We had all worked so hard. I thought about it as I watched more alums walk into the gym. Sure, we wanted to give a great party. But that wasn't the reason we threw ourselves into it with such eagerness and enthusiasm.

I think it was a serious distraction from the horrible murders, from all the nightmares we had been living through.

I watched the Linden grads entering the gym and gazing around at the posters and other nineties decorations.

They were all in their thirties. Most of them looked their age, or even older. Some of the men had bald spots on the tops of their heads and stomachs poking over their belts.

The women were mostly in better shape, although some looked tired, maybe from being parents.

A few couples began to dance immediately in the center of the floor. I saw a lot of handshakes and people introducing each other. Some couples mingled a little awkwardly. I guessed they hadn't seen each other in a while.

Name tags. The word popped into my head.

There were supposed to be name tags for everyone. I glanced to the name tag table in front of the entrance. No one there. "Morgan." I said her name out loud. Morgan was in charge of name tags.

I trotted over to the food table. "Delia, have you seen Morgan? She isn't at her table."

Before Delia could answer, the double doors swung open and Morgan strutted into the gym. Her coppery hair was down over her shoulders. Perfect. Her green eyes caught the light from the ceiling and sparkled. Her skin looked creamy and pale in the bright light.

A thin smile spread over her face as she moved toward the center of the room. She made such an entrance— she was so stunningly beautiful—people stopped their conversations and turned to look at her.

"Hello, everyone! Hello!" she screamed.

More guests turned to watch her. For some reason, Frankie cut off the music. Voices murmured softly. Then a hush fell over the gym.

"Hello, everyone!" Morgan cried, raising both arms to make sure she had everyone's attention.

What on earth is she doing? I asked myself. I clenched my fists at my sides. My whole body tensed.

What is this about?

"I brought some guests of my own!" Morgan shouted, her voice ringing off the gym walls. "Don't worry. They don't need name tags. They're all DEAD!"

She tossed back her head, her hair flowing down her back, and laughed, a crazy maniacal laugh.

And then the doors pushed open once again—and her friends began to stagger and stumble in.

Screams rang out as we saw their tattered clothes, their decayed bodies, gray faces with patches of skin missing, empty eye sockets. Bony hands, missing legs. Skeletal creatures, stumbling, falling to their bony knees, as if they hadn't walked in a long time.

One after another, a dozen, then a dozen more. And as the grunting, moaning creatures circled the gym, a horrible stench rose up. Sour and disgusting, the smell floated thickly over the room. The smell of rotting flesh, the smell of death.

Gripped in horror, I couldn't move. I stood trembling, my legs like rubber bands, my arms stretched in front of me like a shield. Screams all around me. The odor made my stomach churn. I tried to hold my breath, but the smell was already inside my nostrils.

I opened my mouth, but the scream choked in my throat.

And as the dead guests stumbled and staggered with their empty eye sockets, their grinning skeletal teeth, their missing arms and legs . . . As they circled us, trapping us in their odor, their hideousness, the horror of this scene of living dead . . . Morgan raised her arms in triumph and shouted over the screams:

"Let's party, everyone! Let's party till we *drop*! Ha-ha. It's a carnival. And the freak show has just begun. Who wants to dance with us? Who wants to dance with the DEAD?"

52

DELIA CONTINUES THE STORY

For a few seconds, I could hear only the moans and animal grunts of Morgan's dead guests. But then Frankie cranked up the music again.

This is how we do it!

This is how we do it!

The words repeated like a chant. Freddy's sound system was up so high, I could feel the floor vibrate under my shoes. Alums were screaming in horror, but the music completely drowned them out.

A dead guy in shredded rags, one hand missing, grabbed Amber with his one bony hand. She tried to pull away, but the grinning skeleton was too strong for her. He started to dance a hobbled dance.

Another dead creature wrapped his decayed arms

around one of the alums and pressed his open, lipless mouth to hers. Dead people wrestled a guy to the floor while another one forced his wife to dance.

A few alums were on their knees, throwing up against the gym wall. A bunch of them went hurtling to the double doors, but a line of eyeless dead people blocked their escape.

Fights broke out. An alum punched a dead guy in the face, and the corpse's whole head flew off and bounced over the floor. Headless, he grabbed the alum and they wrestled, punching and pummeling one another.

This is how we do it.

This is how we do it.

The gym was a blur of horror. Wrestling, fighting, screaming, dancing. Zombies. Morgan had emptied the cemetery to bring her guest list, an ugly, stench-carrying crew of zombies.

Why? Why did she do it? I thought I knew. Pure jealousy. She was beautiful but it didn't matter. She was dead and everyone else was alive.

I turned and searched for Julie. I finally found her huddled behind the food table. Zane had appeared. I didn't remember if he was working at the party or not. But there he was. He and Julie were holding each other in a tight hug, their eyes on the madness, on the screaming, squealing terror.

Gripped in shock, the screams and horrified cries ringing in my ears, I thought of Winks. Poor dead Winks. And then I couldn't take it anymore.

Ducking under the grasp of a one-legged zombie, I broke through a crowd and grabbed Morgan by the shoulders. "Why?" I cried. "Why did you do this?"

She made no attempt to free herself from my grasp. Instead, she brought her face close to my ear. "I'm Morgan Fear," she said, her voice hard and cold.

Then with a loud groan, she broke my grip. Her eyes flamed like green fire, and she grabbed my arm with both hands. Her hands felt cold and hard as steel as she jerked me hard, almost pulling me off my feet.

She pulled my hands behind my back and shoved me hard. "Over here, Delia."

"Let go!" I screamed. "Hey—let go!"

She was pulling me to the bleachers at the far end of the gym. "Hey—let go! Morgan—what are you going to do?"

53

DELIA CONTINUES

I twisted and squirmed, but Morgan was too strong for me. I swung my head around and tried to bite her arm. But she lifted me off the floor and carried me to the back of the bleachers.

"Let me go! What are you doing? Let me go!" My cries came out high and shrill, my voice cracking in terror.

She shoved me behind the benches and slammed my back against the tile wall. "Morgan, stop—!" I pleaded.

"Your turn, Delia honey," she said, her green eyes as cold as ice, her voice low and hard. "You've asked for this, dear, and now it's your turn."

"Asked for this?" I choked out. "Asked for what? Morgan, please—"

She lowered her voice to a whisper. "I'm so hungry, Delia. Soooo hungry."

Her eyes rolled up in her head. Her mouth opened wide, revealing long, pointed teeth. She lowered her head quickly.

I gasped as her teeth sank deep into my shoulder. Her hands tightened their grip as the teeth pierced my skin. She began to suck.

I held my breath. The wall was a yellow blur in my eyes.

What am I going to do? What am I going to do?

My only thought. The words repeated in my mind.

What am I going to do?

My whole body jolted as Morgan stopped abruptly and slid her teeth from my shoulder. The light appeared to dim in her eyes as she squinted at me.

She made a sick gagging sound—and shoved me away, pushed me hard into the wall.

Spitting, choking, she swept her hair back off her face. "Omigod! Delia, you—you—" she uttered.

I knew what I had to do. I took a deep, shuddering breath and pushed myself off the wall. I spun away from her and forced my legs to move. My knees wanted to fold. My whole body wanted to collapse.

I wanted to curl up on the floor, curl into a tight ball

where I'd be safe and alone. But I knew what I had to do. I knew. I knew.

The ceremonial Linden Vikings ax was propped in a corner beside the food table. I could see the yellow-and-blue handle tilting against the wall.

I stumbled forward, legs still not wanting to cooperate. I swung both arms forward, prepared to grab the ax handle.

"Delia—come back!" I heard Morgan's harsh command. "Come back here!" in a bellowing voice that sent shivers down my body.

I glanced back to see how close she was. She was running hard, her red hair flying behind her. "Come back, Delia!"

I grabbed the ax handle with both hands. Gripped it tightly. Raised it off the floor. Heavier than I'd imagined. Heavier, the handle long and straight.

I know what I have to do, Morgan.

I know what I have to do.

There's only one way to kill you.

She dove at me, mouth open in an angry roar, hands outstretched to grab me.

I swung the ax, and Morgan screamed.

54

DELIA CONTINUES

Morgan's scream cut off as the ax blade sliced through her neck. No blood spurted out. She had no blood.

People gasped and uttered horrified cries as her head flew high, across the gym, the red hair billowing behind it. A groan escaped Morgan's open mouth.

The head appeared to float for a long time, and then it dropped heavily to the gym floor, bounced twice, and came to a rest on its side.

Around the room, the zombies began to murmur. They were all gaping at the head on the floor. They stood still for a long time, studying it, muttering to each other in ugly tones from deep in their empty bodies.

Then, as if given a signal, they began to disintegrate. Staggering, stumbling, arms shaking at their sides, empty heads bowed, they fell apart, limb from limb. A terrifying thunder echoed through the gym as they cracked and crumbled into piles of dust. Piles of powdery dust, and all that remained was their stench.

I suddenly realized the ax was still gripped tightly in my hands. I gazed at the shiny blade, gazed at it until it seemed to hypnotize me. The handle began to burn in my hands.

What have I done?

I let the ax fall to the floor. Then I dropped to my knees, lowered my head, and shut my eyes. But even with my eyes shut, I still saw that ax blade cutting through Morgan's neck, saw the head go flying, uttering its last groan.

When I finally raised my head, Julie was standing beside me. She had one hand placed on my trembling shoulder. "It's okay, Delia," she whispered. "She's gone. The vampire is gone."

And then I saw Imhoff on my other side.

"I . . . I can't believe I did that," I said to him, barely able to choke out the words. "I can't believe I killed Morgan."

He knelt down beside me and spoke softly, his silvery eyes seeking mine. "You did the right thing, Delia. You didn't kill a human. You must always remember that.

You didn't kill a human. You killed a vampire."

I gazed back at him. I didn't know how to reply.

"You saved a lot of lives," Julie said.

Imhoff nodded. "Yes. Delia, you saved a lot of lives."

I turned and saw that my friends had formed a tight circle around me. "Delia, you're a hero," Julie cried. "You're a hero!"

55

DEAR DIARY,

My emotions today are all over the place, and this is the only way I can get my head straight. Or maybe I never will.

I'm like on a roller coaster. My feelings ride way up up up, and then come crashing down in a screaming heap. I feel ecstatic one minute, triumphant, a winner, on top of the world. The next minute I am filled with regret. Not just regret but hate, hatred of myself and what I did in the gym earlier tonight.

But, Diary, did I have a choice?

No. No choice. No choice at all.

I knew I had to destroy Morgan the moment she sank her teeth into me, prepared to drink her fill, and realized I have no blood.

The shock on her face was worth the whole trip.

She gagged. She was sick when she realized what I was. What I am.

She was sick because she knew I now had no choice. I had to kill her if I was to keep my secret.

If only I'd known sooner that Morgan was the other vampire in Linden. I could have saved Winks— saved him for myself.

I picked Winks out as soon as I arrived here in the fall. I made him feel that I was in love with him. I made everyone feel that I was in love with him. That I needed him. That poor, shy, quiet Delia had attached herself to the Big Guy and wouldn't let go.

Well . . . I didn't want to let go. I was saving Winks for a special treat.

But she spoiled my treat, Diary. Morgan got to him first. She drank half his sweet nectar before he ran out of his cousin's house.

He ran out of that house, into my waiting arms. And I only got half. I drank it so hungrily. The half of Winks's blood that Morgan hadn't consumed.

It left me so hungry, Diary. So achingly hungry. A gnawing that wouldn't stop. A gnawing that tortured my whole body.

Feeding on the funeral director helped me for a few days. He was pretty old but his blood was still sweet and filling. So, yes, Diary, I killed Winks and the funeral man. It is my fate. Why should I go hungry?

And look at me now. I'm a hero!

I killed the vampire and saved everyone's life. Ha.

Everyone loves me now. Poor, quiet, little Delia saved everyone. Delia is a hero.

So . . . I gave myself a little reward.

That strange-looking guy—Cal Imhoff. Big-time vampire hunter with his dark suits and that white-blond hair and silvery eyes that don't look real.

The crazy dude offered to drive me home.

I made him pull over a few blocks from my house. I told him I felt sick. Then I grabbed his head, pulled him down to me, and drank my fill.

Sweet. Very sweet. The blood had a little spice to it, a little kick. I can still taste it on my lips.

A hero deserves a reward, don't you agree, Diary?

Of course, I wouldn't tell this to anyone else.

You're my best friend, Diary. My only best friend. My only real friend. Always remember that.

Love,

Delia

Return to R.L. STINE'S terrifying world of

FEAR STREET

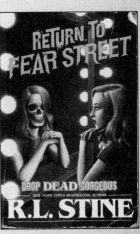

JOIN THE

Epic Reads

COMMUNITY